Trouble on Paradise
An ExForce novella

By Craig Alanson

Craig Alanson

Thanks to my dedicated team of 'beta readers':

Ross Bumpass
John Reed
Mick Wilson
Janet Wolfenden

Cover by Melinda Burt
pixelperfectpublishing@gmail.com

Craig Alanson

Table of Contents

Chapter One
Chapter Two
Chapter Three
Chapter Four
Chapter Five
Chapter Six
Chapter Seven
Chapter Eight
Chapter Nine
Chapter Ten

CHAPTER ONE
Three days after Skippy used maser cannon projectors to destroy the Kristang battlegroup at Paradise

"All zPhones in the bag," Staff Sergeant Surmacz pointed to the sack he held with one hand. A trickle of sweat ran down his forehead and into his left eye; the salt stung his eye. He wiped it away with the back of his free hand, silently cursing the steaming jungle heat of Lemuria, the southern continent where the Ruhar had dumped almost all humans on Paradise. Dumped us here, he thought bitterly, to get us out of the way. Out of sight, and out of mind for the Ruhar civilian population. Stuck in Lemuria, without transportation, without weapons, where primitive humans could not cause problems for the Ruhar government. Far enough away so humans could not threaten the native Ruhar. The Ruhar government had been right about that, when Ruhar starships completely dominated the skies.

And then a Kristang battlegroup arrived in orbit, and everything had changed. Those humans who had remained loyal to the Kristang had renewed hope of the Ruhar being forced to leave Paradise. That happy situation ended three days ago, when giant maser cannons no one had known about had blasted most of the Kristang ships apart, and thrown the strategic situation on the planet into chaos. A chaos that Staff Sergeant Surmacz and his fellow Keepers of the Faith hoped to exploit, to assure the Ruhar did not regain control over the planet humans called Paradise.

"I turned it off, Sergeant." Eric Koblenz waved his zPhone, reluctant to part with his only means of communications beyond shouting range.

"In the bag," Surmacz insisted. "And that wasn't a suggestion soldier, it was an order. You think pressing the 'Off' button really kills the power to a zPhone?"

Eric cast a guilty look at his zPhone. "The light turns off. I should-"

"This is why you shouldn't do the thinking around here, Koblenz," Surmacz tilted his head as if he were speaking to a young and particularly stupid child. "This is alien tech, we don't understand anything about it. You've got a Kristang phone using a Ruhar network. Even if the damned hamsters haven't figured out how to load tracking software into these things, I can guarantee the lizards were listening to everything we said and wherever we went, whether we turned it off or not. Put it in the bag."

"I hadn't thought of that," Koblenz admitted and handed the phone to the sergeant.

Surmacz took the zPhone, checked that it was powered down, and dropped it in the bag. "When's the last time you charged it?"

Koblenz looked surprised by the question. "Never. The lowest it ever showed was an 86% charge."

"And you've had it since Camp Alpha?" Surmacz didn't wait for an answer. "These things pick up energy from motion, from the sun, from your body's electrical field, even from the magnetic field of the planet. We don't ever need to plug them in to keep them charged. That tells me that we humans don't understand this tech at all. We're leaving these here. You heard the orders," he meant word passed down from the informal leadership of the Keeper movement. "From now on, communications are voice only, person to person. Nothing electronic, and nothing in writing. Our enemy," he meant the Ruhar, "can hack any signal we transmit, and crack any encryption we use. Great, that's all of them," Surmacz took the last zPhone, cinched the bag shut and dropped it under a bush. The zPhones were waterproof, he didn't need to worry about them. "Now, we get out of these uniforms. Strip off everything except shorts, boots and socks." He took off his own top.

Eric Koblenz didn't like the idea of walking through the jungle of Lemuria almost naked. "We're going into this op in our underwear?"

"No, Private Koblenz," Surmacz pointed to a trio of dufflebags on the floor. "There's good, honest homemade pants and shirts in those dufflebags, we'll be wearing those. These uniforms are too likely to have tracers attached to them, so they're staying behind."

A soldier named Markey fingered the collar of his uniform top suspiciously. "Sewn into the collars?" He guessed.

Sergeant Surmacz shook his head. "No, that's what we would have to do. With the tech available to hamsters, they could weave nanofibers directly into the fabric anywhere."

"If they can track us, could they be listening to us now?" Markey hurried to get his top and pants off, flinging them across the hut.

"UNEF Intel doesn't think the hamsters are doing that, and that is one thing Keeper leadership trusts UNEF Intel to tell the truth about," Surmacz shook his head. "Since we all usually carry zPhones everywhere we go, the hamsters have no need of any other way to listen to us. They might also be tracing us with our socks or underwear," he gave a rueful grin, "or our boots. That's a risk we'll have to take."

"I'm happy to get out of the UNEF gear," Markey grimaced. Some of them, Markey included, had all already removed the UNEF patches from their uniforms when UNEF Command on Paradise traitorously considered declaring allegiance to the Ruhar. The Keeper movement got a significant boost three days before, when mysterious maser cannons blasted the Kristang battlegroup and chased the remaining ships away from Paradise! Rumors were flying around that humans, UNEF, were involved somehow in a treacherous sneak attack on humanity's allies. That had been the final straw for many people who were on the fence about joining the Keeper movement, or were lukewarm about their commitment to the Keeper cause. For humans to take up arms, against the species who protected Earth from the Ruhar, was too much for the Keepers not to take action. Direct action. It was time, Keeper leaders had declared in clandestine meetings, to act. An attack on UNEF headquarters? That idea had been discarded because humans killing humans was not likely to impress the Kristang. And because not even the most fanatical Keeper wanted to kill other humans. The best option for Keeper action would be to hit the Ruhar directly, but since humans were isolated on the southern continent of Lemuria, hitting the Ruhar was impractical. Keeper leadership was at a loss for ideas, until UNEF received notice from the Ruhar that there were several potential projector sites on Lemuria. The Ruhar would be investigating, and working to reactivate, projectors on Lemuria. What they wanted UNEF to do was to stay the hell out of their way. Rumor had it that neither the Ruhar nor the Kristang controlled the projector network, which UNEF HQ was trying to make sense of. According to another rumor, there were dozens of other projectors sites around the planet that neither the Ruhar nor Kristang had found yet; both sides were frantically deep scanning the surface to find the hidden projectors.

Immediately following the Ruhar message, the Kristang had sent a message to UNEF command, stating that they also would be flying over Lemuria. The Kristang would be trying to find and reactivate projectors for their own use, and trying to seize control of, or destroy projectors that were under Ruhar control. The Kristang had angrily demanded that their human UNEF allies resist the Ruhar, and assist Kristang efforts to take control of projectors. UNEF Command responded to both Ruhar and Kristang that humans were effectively neutrals in the current fight; an easy decision since unarmed humans couldn't do much anyway.

It was an easy decision for the Keepers also. They did not have to find a way to travel all the way to the northern continent to hit a Ruhar target, the Ruhar were coming to them in Lemuria! According to the Kristang, the Ruhar had identified a hidden projector site less than forty miles from a UNEF village, on the western edge of UNEF territory. The Ruhar had flown a team there to excavate the site and bring the projector back online, and that was expected to take at least several days. During that time, the Ruhar team on the surface would be vulnerable. This was the big opportunity the Keepers had been looking for; a chance to hit the Ruhar directly and do something useful to help their Kristang allies. If Keepers could attack the projector site, they could delay the Ruhar effort to reactivate the weapon. Possibly even force the Ruhar to retreat long enough for the Kristang to arrive and take over. Attacking the Ruhar at the closest projector site would be the most useful action humans could perform on Paradise, since the time Sergeant Bishop and his team shot down a pair of Ruhar Whale dropships. No way were the Keepers going to miss what was likely to be a one-time-only opportunity. Staff Sergeant Surmacz had been contacted by Keeper leadership; the message was written in code on paper and hand delivered by courier. Surmacz burned the paper immediately after reading it. Then he gathered a team of volunteers. Their mission, and the mission of four other similar teams, was not to attack the Ruhar yet. They couldn't attack effectively, as they had no weapons other than spears, bows and arrows, and shovels with sharpened blades. Surmacz's mission was simple: a raid on a UNEF security patrol to acquire weapons. Once the Keepers had weapons, real weapons like M-4 rifles, some of the Keepers would create chaos and distractions, while the main team hit the Ruhar projector site.

When the team was dressed in their new clothes that had been hand-made from old tents and whatever other fabric was available, Surmacz led them out the back of the hut and straight into the jungle. There was a cache less than half a mile inside the jungle, with such weapons as were available, and backpacks that were distressingly light on food. They had packs of dehydrated soup made from vegetables and fruit, some dried fruit, and bread that had been baked hard as a cracker. In the heat and humidity of the jungle, Surmacz expected even the tough bread to start going bad quickly. No matter, they had enough food for the planned length of their mission plus two days, on lean rations. They could manage.

"You heard?" Captain Chisolm asked as he burst through the door of the hut. He removed his camouflage patrol cap and shook it in the doorway to get rid of the water from the jungle rainstorm. Chisolm was careful with the cap; it was the only one he had left. No more supplies were coming from Earth, UNEF HQ on Paradise was not issuing any gear to Keepers like him.

"Yes, Sir," Sergeant Robinson acknowledged, holding up his zPhone. "The message was directed at us," he meant the Keeper village, "by now the whole planet will have heard. Are we going, Captain?"

"I am. This will be volunteers only, Sergeant. The Kristang asked for fifty men, men only," he grimaced at the need to comply with their allies' prohibition against women in combat. Against women in pretty much any military role. There weren't many women in the village; as a percentage of inhabitants, the Keeper villages had even less women than the general UNEF population. But excluding women made it more difficult for Chisolm to round up enough volunteers. "My guess is fifty of us is the max they can cram aboard whatever transport they're sending." After the massive air battle now called The Great

Paradise Furball several days ago, neither side had enough aircraft to establish air superiority, and barely even enough to support ground troops.

"Sir," Robinson glanced away, then met the Captain's eyes. "Do you believe the Kristang? That they really need us to support an assault on a Ruhar projector site?"

Chisolm's eyes narrowed. Robinson was one of his most trusted, steady men. If Robinson was questioning their lizard-like allies, many others in the village were also likely having second thoughts. Declaring continued loyalty to the Kristang and disgust with UNEF was easy to say. Actually going into combat against the Ruhar was the real test of whether humans on Paradise would be Keepers of the Faith.

"We've been lied to so many times, I'm questioning everything I've been told, Sir," Robinson stated flatly. "We don't have weapons, we've not been trained to fight alongside the Kristang, and we'll be attacking a position the Ruhar will have had time to prepare for a static defense. The Kristang probably want to avoid damaging this projector, so we won't be allowed to use artillery, which we don't have anyway."

"The Kristang will provide weapons," Chisolm said hopefully. The message had not included that detail. The message overall had been short in details, being devoted mostly to taunting and insulting humans as being wholly unworthy of being considered allies by the glorious Kristang. This, in a message that ordered the Keeper village to provide fifty volunteers. Captain Chisolm was determined to remain loyal to his original pledge to the Kristang; that didn't mean he was not aware their communications skill could use some improvement. "The Kristang never trained us to fight alongside them, because they are super warriors; they never thought we would be of any use to them in combat. Humans are too short, too slow, too weak to keep up with Kristang troops. They gave us the evac mission here, because all we had to deal with was hamster civilians, and we almost screwed that up anyway."

Robinson nodded but he didn't look happy. "I'll go if you go, Sir. Scraping together fifty volunteers quickly might be a tall order. Most of these people haven't done any combat training in a long time."

"None of us have," Chisolm agreed. "We've been too busy trying to feed ourselves." He almost added 'no thanks to the Kristang'. "Talk to people, Sergeant, I'm going to meet with as many people as I can. Major Gomez wants as many volunteers as possible; it would be great if the entire village is waiting when the Kristang transport arrives. That's in," he checked his zPhone, "less than two hours."

When the Kristang transport arrived, it was trailing smoke from one engine, and set down heavily in the middle of a corn field, skidding and plowing up several meters of precious crops. If people had known the Kristang would treat a critical human food source so carelessly, there may have been even less than the forty seven volunteers waiting. The transport was distressingly small, Captain Chisolm did not see how fifty humans could possibly fit inside, nor how such an overloaded transport could manage to take off. Major Gomez, who would be staying behind because a tree had fallen and broken one of his legs, gave Captain Chisolm a questioning look. Then Gomez regained his composure and drew himself upright. His people were already uncertain about the situation; he could not show his own fears.

The rear ramp of the transport swung down, and two Kristang in body armor panels stepped out, waving the waiting humans forward. The front rank hesitated until Major Gomez saluted them and pointed to the transport. Then, with a shout that was less loud and enthusiastic than Gomez hoped for, the front rank trotted forward and up the ramp.

Gomez then turned and saluted Captain Chisolm. "Captain, good luck to you."

Trouble on Paradise

"I will return with my shield, or on it," Chisolm said with grim determination.

Gomez suppressed a frown at Chisolm's melodramatics. "Just remember, Captain, your mission isn't to win the battle for the Kristang; it is to demonstrate to our allies that humans are steadfast and reliable in combat. No one expects your men to take on the Ruhar by yourselves."

"Yes, Sir," Chisolm's expression reflected his excitement. He started to run forward, and turned to say something, but whatever sentiment he intended to convey was drowned out by the booming voice of a Kristang, amplified by the transport's external speakers.

"Human! We ordered fifty of your men to be provided to us. We count forty seven," the translated voice still conveyed outrage.

"We are," Gomez looked around, mortified. He had ordered all other people not going with the Kristang to stay out of sight, but human nature being what it was, curiosity had gotten the better of many people. Gomez himself, with his right leg in a splint and him leaning on crutches, was clearly not capable of combat. The people peeking around huts, or lingering at the edge of the field, were not doing humanity any favors. What could he say? That some among the Keepers of the Faith did not want to go into battle with their patrons? "You have our finest-"

"Give us three more, or we will take them from you!" The Kristang's voice demanded. The two Kristang at the bottom of the ramp stopped urging humans aboard, and unslung their rifles.

Gomez spoke as loudly as he could, hoping his people would respond. Since they had broken with UNEF, the Keepers had kept to a military hierarchy, but Gomez knew he really had only as much authority as his people wanted to give him. Ordering three people to their likely deaths was probably not within his power. "Keepers of the Faith! We need three true warriors to step up and prove that humans do not cower from the prospect of battle! Prove to the aliens who rescued our home planet from invasion! Three people!" There was movement at the edge of the field, people shuffling their feet and talking to each other, but no one had yet stepped forward. Gomez feared the two Kristang soldiers would charge across the field, grab three of his people and start shooting the others. He opened his mouth to openly plead for volunteers, but just then, three men who had been huddled and talking animatedly with each other, stepped forward and began slowly jogging across the field. Jogging as if at any moment, they would surrender to their fears and stop. "Warriors of Earth!" Gomez shouted. "We salute you!"

The Major's salute was picked up by the people ringing the field, and if the three had any doubts, they squashed them and continued forward until they reached the bottom of the transport's ramp. There, the two hulking Kristang prodded them forward with the muzzle of their rifles. The Kristang shuffled forward until they disappeared into the transport. The ramp closed, and the transport took off unevenly, dragging itself forward then flying low, churning up and destroying crops as it flew. Black smoke poured from one engine, before the engine sound changed and the smoke became thin and white. The transport gained speed rapidly, and was lost from sight beyond the jungle trees.

Gomez shuddered. Fifty people, all good people; people who had sacrificed their futures in order to protect the billions of humans on Earth. He did not expect to ever see them again.

"We wait here," Surmacz held up a hand to halt the column the next afternoon. "What's up, Sergeant?" Koblenz asked quietly.

"We have to cross a river, so we'll be marching along this road," he pointed ahead to a bright line across their path. A place where there was a gap in the dense interlocking canopy of trees overhead. The jungle concealed the marchers from satellites, although everyone expected Ruhar sensor technology would not be degraded by something as simple as tree cover. The purpose of staying off the roads was to avoid UNEF troops who might be using the roads. "The road has a bridge across the river. We wait here until an hour before dark, then we cross the bridge. To save you from asking me more stupid questions, Koblenz, we are waiting because there is a regular UNEF patrol that drives along this road every afternoon. After those hamvees pass by, we get on the road and cross the bridge."

"We're not going to ambush that patrol?" Markey asked.

"No," Surmacz shook his head. "Too hard a target for us; they'll be inside their hamvees. We don't have anything," he pointed to the collection of crude weapons carried by the team, "that can penetrate that glass the hamsters use." Surmacz knew that in the steamy afternoon heat of the jungle, the patrol would have their hamvee windows rolled up and the air conditioning on. The 'glass' of hamvee windows was a tough clear composite material that an arrow or spear, even a large rock, would bounce right off. On Camp Alpha, Surmacz had seen a demonstration that a hamvee window could stop a 9MM round at close range. He remembered being amazed that a 9MM round left no more mark on the window than if a large bug had hit the window at highway speed. The standard 5.66MM NATO round from an M4 rifle didn't fare much better against the Ruhar glass; it took an explosive-tipped Kristang round to punch through the composite. And the Kristang advised more than one hit was needed to be sure to make a hole in the 'glass'. "We'll let those boys ride right by us."

After their forward lookout reported that three UNEF hamvee patrol vehicles had rolled by, the Keeper team tentatively stepped out onto the road. Sergeant Surmacz had assured them there were no UNEF soldiers nearby so they could talk normally, but most people were walking without speaking. Early evening in the jungle of Lemuria reminded Eric Koblenz of a summer evening back home. Towering clouds were tinged orange and golden by the rays of the setting sun. Insects were already buzzing or chirping on both sides of the road. The typically gusty midday wind had died down and the air was absolutely still, without even a breath of a breeze. The thunderstorms that rolled across the jungle every afternoon like clockwork had been brief that day, so that the dirt road had quickly dried out, and boots kicked up puffs of dust as they marched. It was peaceful, and by unspoken agreement, people didn't want to break the quiet that wrapped around them like a comforting blanket. Or, they were all lost in thought, and maybe many of them were thinking of home; a planet they would probably never see again.

"You're quiet," Markey nudged Koblenz and almost whispered. "What's going on with you? You're usually a freakin' motormouth."

Eric Koblenz looking guiltily toward Staff Sergeant Surmacz. "Does this sit right with you?"

"What part of it?" Markey answered quietly. "Being on another planet? Or the planet being controlled by the enemy? Or that the Ruhar may not be our enemy?"

"Shit," Koblenz's breathed out a defeated sigh. "All of that. This is way too freakin' complicated. I'm a soldier, I have a rifle. Point me toward a target and I'll do my duty. Out here, I'm being asked to decide who the enemy is."

Trouble on Paradise

"We can't tell the enemy from the good guys?" Markey shrugged. "Hell, the US Army has been fighting that way since Vietnam, ain't nothing new. Iraq, Afghanistan, Nigeria; all the Hajis look the same."

"Yeah, I guess. Here, the Hajis are us."

"How you figure that?"

"We're not marching to attack the hamsters; we're on our way to hit humans. UNEF or not, they're humans. Humans could get killed, by other humans. How fucked up is that?"

Markey nodded. "F'ed up for certain, man."

"I'm doing what I think is the right thing, but," Eric grimaced and looked up at a cloud. Surprisingly, it had rained only briefly that day, and the air was suffocatingly hot. "I came all the way out here to do my duty, and if UNEF HQ ever reports back to Earth, they'll say I went Elvis on them," he said sadly, using slang for a soldier absent without leave.

"Hey," Markey gripped Koblenz's shoulder reassuringly. "We didn't go over the hill on UNEF; they abandoned their mission on us."

Koblenz looked sadly down at his dusty boots. "We're in a jungle, on an alien planet, and I must be homesick, because this reminds me a lot of home. You know, walking down a dirt road on a summer afternoon, kicking up dust. Coming back from a swimming hole, or fishing, or whatever. Walking home," he blinked to clear tears from his eyes. "Damn," he wiped his eyes with the back of a hand, "this dust is getting to me."

"Yeah, the dust," Markey agreed, suddenly thinking of his own home in Kentucky. Thinking of when he was a boy, walking along the dirt road behind his parents' house. Walking with a group of friends, coming back from a creek where there was a deep pool of water perfect for cooling off on a hot summer day. "Where's home for you?"

"West Virginia," Koblenz answered. "My folks have a place up in a holler, that's a valley-"

"I'm from eastern Kentucky, I know what a holler is," Markey had to blink away his own tears. "West Virginia, huh?"

"Almost heaven," Koblenz said with a quickly fading grin.

"I've been there, my mother's parents are from Beckley."

Koblenz nodded. "I miss it. And now I think I'm never going to see it again."

Markey watched Eric Koblenz hang his head miserably, staring at his boots as they marched. Markey patted the other soldier on the back, and began to sing softly. "*Almost heaven, West Virginia. Blue Ridge Mountains, Shenandoah river. Life is old there-*"

Koblenz joined him, neither of them having any talent for singing and not caring. "*-older than the trees. Younger than the mountains, blowin' like the breeze.*"

Six other soldiers around them picked up the familiar chorus, singing louder. "*Country roads, take me home, to the place I belong. West Virginia, mountain momma. Take me home, country roads.*"

Then the whole column sang, even Sergeant Surmacz. "*All my memories gathered 'round her. Miner's lady, strangers to blue water. Dark and dusty, painted on the sky, misty taste of moonshine, teardrops in my eye. Country roads, take me home, to the place I belong. West Virginia, mountain momma. Take me home, country roads-*"

When they finished the last chorus, even Surmacz had tears in his eyes. "Ah, dammit, now you guys have got me going."

"Where's home for you, Sergeant?" Markey asked.

"Alabama," Surmacz said wistfully. And of course, that started the entire group singing *Sweet Home Alabama,* making Sergeant Surmacz have to join in.

Captain Chisolm sat rigid with his back to a rock, trying to control his ragged breathing. There was a soldier to his right and one to his left, also gasping for air as quietly as possible. All three of them gripped their Chinese rifles so tightly their knuckles were white; Chisolm knew that was bad practice, he also couldn't order his own fingers to ease their grip at the moment.

Chisolm and two others. As far as he knew, they were the only survivors of the fifty humans and six Kristang who launched the assault on the Ruhar-held projector site. The display in the Kristang goggles he wore, connected to his zPhone, showed less than sixteen minutes had passed since the dropship landed and fifty four warriors raced out to charge the Ruhar position. Because the dropship had been forced to fly low and land behind a hill to avoid Ruhar antiaircraft missiles, the landing zone had been a kilometer and a half from the Ruhar forward positions. To make contact with the enemy, Chisolm and the other humans had to run over a kilometer, uphill, through dense jungle in the steaming heat. In what Chisolm took as a bad omen, the sky had opened as a brief storm pounded the area with rain, almost as soon as his feet stepped off the aircraft's ramp.

The assault plan, as explained by the Kristang during the rough flight as they were all crammed in the back of the aircraft, was simple. Captain Chislom and the forty nine other humans would charge straight at the Ruhar, making as much noise and causing as much havoc and confusion as possible. Three of the Kristang, wearing awe-inspiring powered armor suits, would swing around to the right, hoping to outflank the Ruhar defenders and gain direct access to the shaft being dug down to the projector. The two Kristang pilots, no doubt knowing they were on a certain suicide mission, brought their aircraft in fast and low from the left, strafing the Ruhar positions but being careful not to hit the projector site.

The sixth Kristang, who had the misfortune of not having a powered armor suit, went up the center with the humans. Officially, the Kristang with the humans was there to provide leadership and guidance on tactics. In reality, he was there to 'encourage' the untrusted humans to attack with true warrior spirit. Chisolm quickly saw that meant their Kristang guide shooting in the back anyone who hesitated even slightly. The first victim to fall was a soldier who stopped running forward because of a large tree down across his path. After first trying to climb over the log and slipping on the mossy growth that covered the rotting trunk, the soldier fell back to the ground and backed up two steps to go around the worst of the tangled branches. That momentary retreat of two steps earned the human a single shot to the back of his head. Chisolm had been startled to hear the distinct report of a Kristang rifle, and turned just in time to see the now headless soldier's body slumping forward.

Captain Chisolm was not the only human to have second thoughts about their forced alliance with the Kristang right then. And he was not the only one to consider turning his own rifle on the vicious Kristang; Chisolm saw several rifle muzzles begin to swing toward their Kristang 'leader'. "Keepers! Forward!" Chislom found himself shouting to his own surprise, years of Army training taking over and saving his life for a few more minutes. The Kristang was not wearing a powered armor suit, but he was a genetically-enhanced super warrior who had a better than even chance to shoot first at anyone who pointed a rifle in his direction. And he was wearing some sort of composite armor panels covering his torso, head, arms and thighs. Chisolm's brain had taken in all those facts as he decided without thinking to continue the charge rather than shooting in rage at their 'leader'.

Trouble on Paradise

That particular Kristang was satisfyingly dead as Chislom huddled behind the rock, working up the oxygen and courage to stand up and run forward. Chisolm had seen the Kristang die, sliced apart and burned by masers. The Ruhar preferred directed-energy weapons to kinetic rounds, although their rifles also could fire explosive-tipped darts that were propelled by an undermounted railgun. To defeat the masers and particle beams of their usual enemy, Kristang armor was designed to flake and ablate away when struck by a beam, protecting the user. The armor could not hold up against being struck by multiple beams, nor could it stop beams from penetrating gaps in the armor. The Kristang had gone down when a maser cooked his shoulder through a gap in the armor. As his head tilted back, another maser had deflected off his chest armor and searing energy seeped through the seam between the chest armor and the neck of his helmet. Seeing the Kristang's skull being boiled from inside and then exploding against the faceplate of his helmet had been both horrifying and satisfying at the same time for Chisolm. Then Chisolm had no more time for reflection, as the jungle was crisscrossed by masers and he needed all his attention to stay alive.

The attack had been a disaster from the start, although Chisolm had been surprised by the poor performance and lack of coordination by the Ruhar defenders. As soon as the ground team left the aircraft and began running through the jungle, the Kristang launched handfuls of miniature flying drones, to counter the Ruhar drones that were already in the air. The fierce drone battle lasted less than a minute as Chisolm and his fellow soldiers ran through the jungle, fearfully glancing at the sky. When the drones finished tangling across the sky, neither side had a single functional drone in the air.

The two Kristang pilots were the first to die from enemy action; their aircraft had barely cleared a hilltop to begin strafing the Ruhar when they were hit simultaneously by four of the six missiles launched by the Ruhar. The burning wreckage of the aircraft cartwheeled through the jungle, knocking down trees and sending splinters flying in every direction. Not a single splinter of wood reached the Ruhar positions; the sacrifice of the aircraft had been for nothing. The air power portion of the assault was an utter failure, except that once the Ruhar no longer faced a threat from above, they seemed unsure of what to do. During the flight in, Kristang had told Chisolm and his fellow Keeper soldiers that the Ruhar were overly reliant on air power and seldom practiced ground-only fighting tactics. This fact was the chief hope of the six Kristang to take on a Ruhar prepared defense, with only the support of fifty primitive humans.

"Ready?" Chisolm asked the soldiers on either side of him, and they both nodded in quick, jerky motions reflecting their fear. Chisolm checked the magazine of his Chinese Army QBZ-95 rifle. Somewhere, the Kristang had gotten access to Chinese weapons, and that is what they provided to Chisolm and his team. Few of the Keepers had ever handled such a weapon, and Chisolm had found the 'bullpup' style rifle, with its curved magazine behind the trigger, to be awkward. He kept bashing the magazine into his hip, and it was difficult to fire from a prone position. At least the Kristang had provided plenty of explosive-tipped ammo of the funky 5.8MM size used by the Chinese rifle. Chisolm ejected the half-empty magazine and inserted a full one, figuring he would not have enough time remaining in his life to swap magazines in combat. He took three deep, calming breaths and prepared to order a final assault. The purpose of the attack by three humans would not be to take the Ruhar position. They had no hope of accomplishing that. What they could accomplish would be to demonstrate to Kristang, across their star-spanning empire, that human allies could and would fight to the death.

Perhaps the assault never had a chance, Chisolm thought as he steeled himself to stand. The three Kristang in powered armor had all been killed without succeeding in outflanking the Ruhar defensive positions around the excavation site. Rather than the wave of human cannon fodder providing cover for the armored Kristang, the opposite had happened. Apparently, the Ruhar commander quickly decided three armored Kristang warriors were a greater threat than a group of lowly humans. That decision, and the poorly-coordinated, hesitant response by the Ruhar, were the reason Chisolm and two others were still alive. Why they had gotten within fifty meters of the Ruhar defensive line. Gotten close enough that Chisolm had seen the excavation site through the jungle, before raking fire that killed a dozen others forced him to momentarily take cover behind the rock.

Cruel as their Kristang 'leader' had been in shooting or stomping to death anyone who failed to run absolutely flat-out through the jungle, Chisolm saw the wisdom in the tactic of simply rushing forward as fast as possible. Their only hope for success, for survival, was to catch the Ruhar off guard, to hit them and be upon their defensive line before the hamsters could adjust to the surprising threat.

That fact of speed being preferable to cover was still true as Chisolm huddled behind the rock. In the few seconds they had taken cover there, the Ruhar could have outflanked them. Chisolm had seen Ruhar soldiers run, and they could seriously move, even burdened by weapons and their own body armor panels. "We go on three. Three, two, GO!" Chisolm shouted, springing to his feet and running. He collided shoulders with the soldier to his left, making both of them stumble for a step as the soldier to their right was cut down by a pair of maser beams. Chisolm had barely time to trip over a tree root before a rocket exploded at the feet of the other soldier, throwing the man's body into Chisolm. Captain Chisolm fell, losing grip on his rifle, then his helmet slammed into a tree trunk.

CHAPTER TWO

Four days after Skippy used maser cannon projectors to destroy the Kristang battlegroup at Paradise

General Marcellus, acting chief intelligence officer for UNEF HQ, remained soberly silent after the conclusion of the briefing from the Ruhar officer. The briefing, given by an angrily resentful Ruhar officer, had been ordered by Deputy Administrator Logellia. The Ruhar military had already been embarrassed and angry about the content of the briefing; to air their dirty laundry in front of two humans was almost too much to bear. Seated beside Marcellus, US Marine Corps General Bailey was also silent, mulling over in his mind what they had learned during the previous thirty seven minutes.

What they had learned was that the Ruhar were not perfect, fantastically advanced though their genetically engineered bodies and their technology were. Their super soldiers were not invincible. Based on their performance in the battle during which a well-armed Ruhar security team had nearly been overrun by six Kristang and fifty humans, the Ruhar were not even competent ground troops. Marcellus thought that, if the battle had been a wargame and he had commanded the defense as an Army captain, he would have received a scathing chewing out by his superiors afterward, and been sent for remedial training in infantry warfare tactics.

"This is very embarrassing," the Deputy Administrator admitted, breaking the depressing silence. Compared to primitive humans, Ruhar soldiers were supposed to be super warriors, with advanced weapons and enhanced biology through genetic engineering. "My military advisors tell me our troops, and our training, are not coping well with ground warfare. We may have become too reliant on air power; our forces have been slow to adapt to combat that is restricted to the ground." She held her hands palms up. "You must understand, warfare where neither side has orbital bombardment capability, or air power, is highly unusual in this conflict. The Kristang have a slight advantage in this type of combat; because of their constant fighting between clans, they practice ground combat frequently. Fighting between clans often happens in crowded urban areas, where neither side can risk using air power or heavy weapons."

Marcellus looked at Bailey, who tilted his head. "Administrator Logellia," Marcellus offered, "we may be able to help you. Our forces are very well trained in ground combat-"

"Bart," Bailey interrupted. "Can we talk privately?"

"Excuse us for a moment, please," Marcellus asked Logellia, before he and Bailey walked out into the corridor.

Keeping his voice low, though aware the Ruhar could listen if they really wanted to, Bailey shook his head. "I thought the official UNEF position is we are neutral in this battle?"

"That ship sailed over the horizon, when a bunch of dumb-fuck Keepers joined the Kristang and killed Ruhar," Marcellus explained. "If we don't demonstrate that the Ruhar can trust UNEF, at least trust UNEF HQ, we're going to be in big Goddamn trouble."

"And if we do throw ourselves into the fight on the side of the Ruhar, and the Kristang take this planet back?"

"Nick, we are thoroughly fucked anyway if the lizards take Paradise," Marcellus declared. "Helping the Ruhar now won't make the lizards hate us any more than they already do. But it might make a big difference in how the Ruhar treat UNEF once the fighting is over. All I'm talking about for now is a few human observers riding along on a Ruhar raid. See how the Ruhar fight, maybe we can give them advice. Hell, fighting desperate ground battles with inadequate resources is the US Marine Corps specialty, isn't it?"

"Ooh-rah," Bailey muttered. "All right, if you can persuade HQ to allow us to ride along, I'm in. Damn, I'd love to see Ruhar troops in action. All I've seen of Ruhar combat tactics so far is sims provided by the Kristang. Now that we know the lizards are lying MFers, I don't know if anything they told us is true."

The next night, Staff Sergeant Surmacz and his team approached a small village, small even by the standards of UNEF on Paradise. The village had been planned to be larger, but the nearby river flooded out the first planting of crops, and it had been decided moving the residents was easier than building a flood control barrier. Now only four people stubbornly clung to the huts they had constructed, tending the fields farthest from the river. The UNEF security patrol stopped in that village only because it was conveniently located at the point where they had to turn around at nightfall, and because the empty huts provided a convenient place to sleep without having to set up tents.

Sergeant Surmacz had been directed to the village because the UNEF security team was known to stop there overnight. With the village being on the edge of UNEF territory, the patrol team was casual about security at night, according to a rumor heard by a Keeper. Surmacz was counting on that rumor being true, and he was counting on human nature. At the end of a long, boring day on patrol, and in the middle of nowhere, the temptation would be for the security team to not make a lot of effort to lock their weapons away. They would likely bring some weapons into the huts with them, but keep the other weapons in their hamvees. To get into a locked hamvee, Staff Sergeant Surmacz had homemade explosives; supposedly enough to blow a hole in a window so someone could reach in and unlock a door. Supposedly the explosive was also not powerful enough to blow up the hamvee and its powercells; Surmacz had to trust the chemist's word on that. To grab the weapons out of a hamvee quickly after blowing a window, his team needed to be close to the hamvee when the explosive detonated. They would not have a large margin for error, and no backup. "After we get the door open, we grab whatever weapons we can find. Priority is heavy weapons, I don't have to explain that to you. If this goes south, we split up and meet at the rendezvous point sundown tomorrow," Surmacz reminded his team. If the operation were to fail, Surmacz thought his team might be hunted from the air by Ruhar aircraft equipped with sensors that could see right through the jungle canopy. According to the Kristang, the massive air battle that was already being called The Great Paradise Furball had destroyed most of the Ruhar's airpower, and neither side had starships in orbit at the moment. Surmacz, and the entire Keeper leadership, were counting on the Ruhar not being willing to assign their precious remaining air assets to tracking a few troublesome humans in the jungles of Lemuria.

"You all know what to do?" Surmacz asked and everyone nodded agreement. They had gone over the plan two dozen times so each member of the team knew their assignment. "Excellent. Remember, we don't want any casualties unless absolutely necessary. Anyone fires a shot or an arrow without my order, they'll be left behind. Got that?"

The team advanced through the almost pitchblack jungle, with Surmacz cursing their complete lack of night vision gear. The Ruhar had taken away all the combat-capable toys provided to UNEF by the Kristang, and even had collected the crude night vision gear UNEF had brought from Earth. The various types of zPhone all had a night vision capability but, of course, they couldn't use zPhones for fear of being tracked.

Trouble on Paradise

The team advanced, single file, as stealthily as they could manage while stumbling through dense jungle undergrowth in almost complete darkness. Their only guide in the night was a single light outside a hut in the village ahead. When Surmacz judged they were less than fifty meters from the clearing, he had his team spread out. "Choi, Martinez, you take point-"

"Nobody move!" A woman's voice rang out from the jungle to their left, followed by a single round fired into the air for emphasis. Bright lights clicked on around them, blinding Surmacz's team. Shading his eyes with one hand, Staff Sergeant Surmacz counted six lights, possibly mounted under M4 rifles. "Do not move from where you are!" The unseen voice ordered. "Drop your weapons now, do it *now*."

"Do what she says," Surmacz ordered.

"We're just going to give up?" Markey protested.

"We're going to live to fight another day, you idiot," Surmacz snapped as he dropped his bow and arrow. "We're surrounded by at least a half dozen people armed with M4s at least. They may have this area seeded with Claymores."

"That's a good guess," the voice acknowledged.

"It's what I would do," Surmacz said with grudging respect. "Everyone, do what the woman says. Drop your weapons and put your hands above your heads. This fight is over for us. For now."

Other than collecting their backpacks, spears, bows and arrow, knives and other crude weapons, the UNEF security team didn't do anything to restrain Surmacz's team. They didn't have to, for without the food in their backpacks, they were totally dependent on UNEF for survival. After they were herded into the village, the Keeper team could see they had been ambushed by a British UNEF security team, led by a female lieutenant.

"If you don't mind compromising operational security, how did you know we were coming here?" Staff Sergeant Surmacz asked hopefully.

"Don't mind at all," the lieutenant answered with a grin, her teeth shining brightly in the artificial light. "We didn't know you were coming here, until you passed by the only other places you might target."

"You tracked us," Surmacz said with disgust.

"The whole way." She lifted a boot. "Tracking sensors in our boots, your boots. The hamsters probably have trackers and other sensors in our clothes, but they know we can't go far in this jungle without boots."

"Shit," Surmacz groaned. He had wanted to make footwear, even had a design sketched for wood soles and canvas uppers, but Keeper leadership told him there was no time, they needed to seize the brief window of opportunity while the Ruhar did not have control of the sky. "We had no chance, then."

"No," she shook her head, "you didn't have any chance at all. Thank you, Staff Sergeant, you did provide my team with entertainment and a training exercise; things have been rather dull around here. This will make you feel worse, so I am going to enjoy telling you. Your whole mission was a waste of your time and energy. Shortly after you left, the lizards landed aircraft in several Keeper villages and flew away with volunteers. The lizards are not only short on airpower, they are thin on manpower. They took on volunteers, that's what they called them, to help secure projector sites the lizards are trying to reactivate, and to attack projector sites held by the Ruhar. That's what the lizards said, anyway. UNEF Command reports your fool Keeper brothers are being given light weapons and thrown into hopeless ground assaults against projector sites controlled by the

Ruhar. The one assault they conducted so far was a slaughter; almost all the Keepers dead or wounded, and the Ruhar still hold the position."

"According to the liars at UNEF Command," Markey said, and spat on the ground.

The British woman gave a disdainful shrug. "You don't need to trust the word of UNEF Command. Think for yourself; how would a small group of humans fair against a well-armed Ruhar security team?" The intel report from UNEF Command had privately concluded the Keeper assault had been much more successful than expected by the Ruhar. If the Keepers merely had another dozen soldiers, they might have overrun the projectors site and temporarily seized control of it. If they had even temporary control, they might have been able to damage or even destroy the projector. Or hold it long enough for the Kristang to reactivate the projector and prevent Ruhar starships from approaching the planet. The problem for the Ruhar, UNEF Command concluded, was they were used to relying on air power, and their skills at ground combat had been allowed to atrophy. By contrast, UNEF troops were well accustomed to improvising tactics with limited resources. Humans, especially out among the stars, were experts at dealing with limited resources. The Ruhar had already very grudgingly admitted they might be able to learn something from the primitive species from Earth.

"What's going to happen to us?" Surmacz asked with a warning look at Markey to keep his mouth shut.

"My orders are to transport you to a holding facility-"

"A prison," Koblenz said angrily. "You are the traitors; *you* should be in prison."

The lieutenant ignored his remark. "What happens to you there, I don't know and I don't care. If it were up to me, I would drive you Sleepers to the end of the road," she pointed past the village, to the edge of UNEF territory, "and leave you in the jungle. Instead, my orders are to see that you are fed and receive medical care as needed. I am a soldier, *I* follow orders from the chain of command. Think about that while you have nothing else to do at the holding facility. And think about the fact that the lizards threw your volunteers into a slaughter, with no hope of accomplishing anything."

"That goes for all of us," Surmacz said quietly.

"Staff Sergeant?" She asked.

"All of us," he pointed to her security team. "All humans, all of UNEF, everyone who left Earth. None of us ever had a chance to accomplish anything useful out here. You have a rifle," he pointed to the British Army L85 rifle the lieutenant carried. "The hamsters," he pointed to the sky, "have starships. None of us can do shit out here."

When General Marcellus suggested the Ruhar allow UNEF observers to accompany a Ruhar ground combat force, he intended to send for a hand-picked UNEF team from Lemuria. Instead, because Administrator Logellia enthusiastically embraced the idea immediately, Marcellus and Bailey found themselves hustled aboard a Ruhar combat transport within the hour. "Be careful what you ask for," Bailey muttered under his breath to Marcellus as a resentful group of Ruhar soldiers herded the two humans up the ramp of their transport, an aircraft that had many hurriedly patched holes in its wings and hull. The Ruhar military intel group had learned the Kristang were sending at least two transports full of warriors to raid and capture a recently-discovered projector site. During the intense ground battle, the two humans were stuck inside their transport, safely tucked behind a hill. The location was only theoretically safe, because the Kristang had managed to launch a pair of antiaircraft missiles that popped up over the hill and scanned the area, searching for targets. Both missiles were intercepted by the transport's defensive maser turrets, but warhead debris *pinged* off the hull like hail. The Ruhar pilots gave apologetic looks toward the humans, who both merely shrugged.

Marcellus, and even more so Bailey, chafed at not being outside with the Ruhar assault force. However, with the Ruhar providing virtual reality goggles, even Bailey had to admit he was actually better able to observe the overall battle from inside the transport. The VR goggles, connected to sensors embedded in the helmets and weapons of Ruhar soldiers, allowed the two humans a God's eye view of the Ruhar side of the assault. They could select to see what an individual Ruhar was seeing, or zoom up and watch the battle unfolding from above, as if the dense forest tree canopy were not there.

What Bailey saw and heard did not impress him. It distressed him.

"Well," General Bailey said with a grunt as he and Marcellus walked the battlefield after the last shot had been fired, "this sure was a full-blown clusterfuck of epic proportions. If one of my platoon commanders conducted an assault like this," he moved to nudge the inert body of a Kristang in a powered armor suit.

"Don't!" General Marcellus warned as he grabbed Bailey's arm, pulling the Marine back. "Those powered armor suits are like a shark's jaws; they can hurt you even when they'd dead. When the Ruhar determine a particular suit is really inactive, they paint it with a yellow circle," he pointed to a yellow-painted suit ten meters away.

Bailey tilted his head. "Bart, *that* is something I would find useful in an intel briefing," his tone implied that he rarely found intelligence briefings to be useful.

"Nick, I only learned about it a minute ago. A hamster had to stop me from getting myself killed," he said with an embarrassed grin. "I'm sure that reinforced the hamsters' thinking that we lowly humans don't belong on any battlefield with them."

"Are you kidding me?" Bailey snorted without humor. "You saw what I saw. The Ruhar should have kicked the lizard's scaly asses here easily. Instead, they got thrown back three times before they broke through the Kristang perimeter," he shook his head disgustedly. "And their casualty rate was thirty six percent. That's shameful. If the Kristang had more than twenty minutes to prepare defenses here, the hamsters might have been sent scurrying back to their base with their furry little tails between their legs."

Marcellus almost remarked that Ruhar did not actually have tails. Bailey had a point; the Ruhar assault had almost failed. The two overloaded Ruhar transports, with Marcellus and Bailey riding in cockpit jumpseats as unwanted observers, had landed near the recently discovered projector site only forty minutes after two Kristang aircraft landed. The Kristang had quickly overrun and killed the lightly-armed Ruhar survey team, and had been working to setup a defensive perimeter, when the Ruhar attacked. The battle had seesawed back and forth for almost an hour, with both sides acquitting themselves poorly, before the superior numbers of the Ruhar wore down the Kristang, and were able to get five soldiers behind the Kristang lines. After that, the battle became a frantic, swirling disorganized gunfight of individual soldiers fighting on their own in the thick forest. Marcellus thought he knew the answer; he asked anyway. "You think we can help our furry allies?"

"Help? Bart, supply my people with the fancy weapons and body armor the Ruhar have, and give us back our zPhones and enhanced-vision goggles, and we could have taken the Kristang position here in one assault. Without genetic enhancements. And with a hell of a lot less casualties. Hell, the Ruhar have totally forgotten basic principles of infantry warfare; they are too reliant on airpower. Their fireteams didn't support each other during the advance, they know nothing about overlapping fields of fire, they got bogged down behind cover way too long. We teach Full Spectrum Dominance battle tactics, but we also train our people what to do if our Airedales aren't able to provide support. The Kristang didn't do much better, in my assessment. They had three powered armor suits," he refrained from kicking the nearest example with a boot, "while our Ruhar buddies only had one. The lizards should have used the advantage of those three super suits to sortie out and outflank us; they could have caused all kinds of havoc. Those MFers can run like lighting in those suits, even in a forest. Instead, they wasted those suits on static defense; that idea was a loser from the get-go. What?" While Bailey was talking, Marcellus tried to silently get the Marine's attention, finally resorting to a slashing motion across his throat. Bailey turned around to see a Ruhar officer standing behind him; the Ruhar's nametag read something that might have sounded like 'Tahl' to a human. The Ruhar must have heard most of Bailey's harsh analysis of the Ruhar assault, for the officer's expression was an angry glare. "Hey," Bailey nodded. He knew Marcellus would prefer he offer an apology to the Ruhar, but Bailey's thinking was that he had nothing to lose. "You heard what I have to say, what is your opinion of this Goddamn mess?"

The Ruhar set his jaw and did not speak. Did not speak verbally; his eyes and body language spoke volumes.

"You and I are soldiers," Bailey pointed to his uniform, ignoring that technically he was a Marine. "We can leave the touchy-feely bullshit to civilians, and talk about what really happened here. Or we can be nice and diplomatic and waste our time, while the lizards are kicking your asses all over this planet. *Your* planet."

The Ruhar's intense glare only intensified.

Marcellus set is mouth in a pained grin. "What General Bailey means is-"

"What I mean is," Bailey interrupted, "that we humans have experience in down and dirty ground fighting. We have to, because by your standards, we don't have any technology worth mentioning. Anything above ten meters off the ground, we're hopeless," he held his hands palms up. With the toe of a boot, he scraped a furrow in the rich forest soil. "But here, on the ground, we know how to fight." He stared the Ruhar officer in the eyes. "Fight without orbital fire support, and without air power. You're an infantry officer?"

The Ruhar waited for the translation, and nodded curtly.

"Great. Let's put our heads together, and kick the fucking lizards off this planet."

The Ruhar opened his mouth, then thought better and closed it.

Marcellus filled the silence, before Bailey could continue. "*Orban* Tahl," he used the Ruhar's rank, roughly equivalent to a major in the US Army. "Neither side controls space near this planet, and neither side can rely on air power. The current situation has both sides racing to reactivate and control as many maser projectors as possible. The Kristang are also trying to take, or destroy, enough Ruhar-held projectors to create a safe-fly zone for their ships overhead. If they can knock back projector coverage over one area, they can bring their ships back, and continue to erode projector coverage until they reestablish supremacy in space around Gehtanu. We are in a race against time for control of this planet, and General Bailey is correct; we do not have time for diplomatic niceties. The Deputy Administrator sent us out here because this type of warfare is what humans have experience with. She sent us *here*," he stabbed an index finger at the ground, "because she hoped some Ruhar officers would be professional enough to know when they could use some help. So," he took a deep breath as two Ruhar walked by, carrying a wounded soldier on a stretcher, "if you are happy with your results here today, General Bailey and I can fly back and enjoy the Administrator's hospitality."

"*Or*," Bailey kept his gaze firmly fixed on Orban Tahl, "together we can make the damned lizards wish they'd never tried to take this planet from the people who call this place home." Bailey knew, from a patch on the right shoulder of Tahl's uniform, that he was a native, that he had grown up on Gehtanu.

"*Tah*," Tahl nodded grimly, using the Ruhar word for 'yes'. He held out a hand and Bailey shook it firmly. "Human, there are plenty of Kristang to kill. Why should we," Tahl grinned, showing his incisors, "keep them all to ourselves?"

Beginning that very night, experienced UNEF infantry leaders were assigned to all Ruhar combat teams, whether assaulting a Kristang-held site, or defending a site controlled by the Ruhar. Typically, a UNEF 'observer' team consisted of one commissioned officer and one sergeant, chosen for their infantry experience and the likelihood they would not piss off the Ruhar they were embedded with. UNEF HQ thought that fostering a strong working relationship with the Ruhar military was just as important as helping the Ruhar win a chaotic ground war against the Kristang.

In addition to UNEF supplying 'observers', the Ruhar also reluctantly bolstered their thin manpower by taking on humans as security forces for critical Ruhar sites. These soldiers, chosen for their ability to get along with alien allies, were given human weapons and led by Ruhar officers. Even the most resentful Ruhar soldiers had to admit that having humans filling the role of defending important infrastructure, freed up Ruhar to take action against the Kristang.

UNEF loyalists also took responsibility for another task: cutting off Kristang access to human manpower. The Ruhar were alarmed by Kristang dipping into the pool of Keepers to boost their strength, and at first, the Ruhar assigned precious combat aircraft to prevent Kristang transports from overflying Lemuria. The Kristang took advantage of the Ruhar shifting their severely limited air combat strength, and the Kristang's own few aircraft attacked Ruhar air bases and population centers on the northern continent. UNEF HQ quickly advised the Ruhar that UNEF could prevent Keepers from joining the Kristang; all UNEF needed was for loyal troops to be given weapons so they could surround Keeper villages. Kristang recruitment of Keepers stopped instantly.

Even with enthusiastic help from UNEF, the situation on the ground was still precarious. Both sides had control of projectors; the Ruhar had an advantage in numbers, but the Kristang had reactivated enough projectors that Commodore Ferlant's ships could not safely approach the planet safely. Ferlant advised that if the situation of the ground turned alarmingly against the Ruhar, he would risk his ships in action against the Kristang-held projector sites, but that would be the absolutely last resort.

Then, Ferlant's ships unexpectedly destroyed the Kristang pursuit squadron, and combat power in the space around the planet became nearly evenly matched. Admiral Kekrando swallowed the bitter pill of failure, and agreed to a cease fire. Both sides kept control of the projectors they held, but further activity was halted. UNEF feared the Ruhar would still reach a deal to give Paradise to the Kristang, until a miracle happened, and the Ruhar found priceless Elder artifacts buried near projector sites. Almost overnight, the planet became a vital resource for the Ruhar, and soon a full Ruhar battlegroup hung in orbit. Admiral Kekrando was forced to admit defeat.

And the people of UNEF, trapped on an alien planet over a thousand lightyears from home, began to hope they could not only survive, but thrive.

And, someday, go home.

CHAPTER THREE
One week after the *Flying Dutchman* left the Paradise system

"This s-sucks," Jesse 'Cornpone' Colter rubbed his gloved hands together.

"T-tell me about it," Dave 'Ski' Czajka agreed. The 'it' came out like 'ih', because Ski's numbed mouth had trouble forming hard vowels in the intense cold.

"I'm so f-frozen, my jaw can barely move to t-talk," Jesse complained.

"Me t-too."

Shauna's voice broke in on their zPhone earpieces. "Hey, you two quit complaining, or get back in the Buzzard. You morons decided to go out there."

"Hey, after all the work we did, freezing our asses off up here, I want to see this test, Shauna," Ski said with a defensive tone.

"We can see it just fine from in here where it's warm," she teased.

"Yeah, sure, on a video feed," Cornpone would have liked to put sarcasm into his voice, but his lips were so frozen, he couldn't manage it. For protection in case of accident during the test, Irene had flown the Buzzard behind a hill, to put plenty of hard-frozen ice and rock between the vulnerable aircraft and any flying debris. "I want to *see* it."

"See it? Through goggles what will filter out like 99% of the light?" Shauna's voice had no trouble projecting sarcasm, since she was in the warm and cozy confines of the Buzzard.

"It makes a difference," Jesse insisted stubbornly.

"What did you say?" Shauna asked. "Hold a minute, I couldn't hear you, let me turn down the cabin heater. Irene has it set on 'tropical' in here. I feel like drinking a rum punch."

"If'n I wasn't such a Southern gentleman, I would say that you are an evil, evil woman, Shauna Jarrett."

"And you are *such* a genius for being out there, Jesse Colter."

Jesse cupped his gloved hands in front of his mouth and blew on the gloves, hoping the hot air would warm his lips. It didn't. He removed a glove and blew on his hand, but his hand got cold so quickly, he had to pull the glove back on. It was 12 degrees below zero Fahrenheit in the arctic of Paradise, and he and Dave were laying prone on snowpack, wearing the best cold weather gear the US Army on Paradise had available. He was wearing five pairs of thick socks; two on each foot and another on, someplace else that was very important to Jesse. The arctic gear totally sucked, compared to the clothing used by the Ruhar. In addition to socks, Jesse was wearing long underwear, a long shirt, a sweater, and a parka. Inside his cold-weather boots, cold was seeping through the socks. The thick fleece cap was keeping his head mostly warm under the helmet. The helmet wasn't for protection in combat, because with a Ruhar battlegroup now based at Paradise, there was no longer any prospect of combat on or around the planet. He wore the helmet for safety, and as protection against the arctic wind. What was really making him cold, worse even than the gusty wind, was lying on the concrete-hard snow. Jesse and Dave had brought seat cushions from the Buzzard; the thin cushions only delayed the cold seeping through from underneath them.

To Jesse's left, a pair of Ruhar were also lying prone on the snow, wearing clothes no heavier than humans would wear on a nice brisk Fall afternoon on Earth. The difference was, the hamster clothing was super high-tech nanofibers, with heaters and cooling tubes woven in. The two hamsters were happily chatting with each other, snacking on what looked like a type of energy bar. Seeing the Ruhar eating what might as well have been a candy bar made Jesse's stomach rumble with hunger. He pressed the mute button on his zPhone and turned to look at Dave. "Shauna may be right about us being stupid for staying out here."

"You wanna go in?" Dave asked hopefully. It had been his idea to watch the test from outside, and now he was regretting Jesse's agreement.

"No, man. At this point, Shauna will think I'm a wimp for backing out now," Jesse lamented with a shake of his head. "I got to keep up my tough-guy image."

"You do realize I can hear you?" Shauna asked.

"Oh, shit!" Jesse's cheeks grew red even in the cold. "Damn it, I pressed the mute button!"

"No," Shauna explained, "your fingers must be frozen. You pressed the 'broadcast' button. Everyone in the area can hear you."

To Jesse's left, the shoulders of the two Ruhar were shaking as if the aliens were laughing. Because they were laughing, at him. One of the hamsters glanced at him, then turned away to say something to her companion. They both exploded with laughter.

"Hey, glad I could entertain y'all," Jesse said sourly. Holding up his zPhone, he carefully set it back on the private channel, that was supposed to be used only by the human crew. All zPhone communications rode on the hamster network, so nothing humans said via zPhone was truly private, but it was better than broadcasting everything, all the time. "Darn it, now I really feel like a freakin' idiot. Come, on Ski, no point freezing out asses off out here."

"Too late," Shauna warned with a giggle she couldn't suppress. "Less than thirty seconds to ignition. You need to stay where you are."

"Shit," Ski said under his breath. "Cornpone, next time I get a stupid-ass idea like this, don't enable me."

"Oh, like this is *my* fault?"

"I never said-"

"Ten seconds, cut the chatter," their pilot Irene ordered from the Buzzard's cockpit.

Dave and Jesse adjusted their Ruhar-supplied goggles, and replied with a silent thumb's up to the two Ruhar.

"-three, two, one, ignition!"

The sky was the color of dull steel; sky and distant snowpack blending so there was no horizon to be seen. The only feature to break the monotony of the landscape was a mountain of dirty snow and black rock, forty miles away. On top of the mountain was a tower with a beacon that blinked alternating yellow and blue; flashing a bright strobe light every seven seconds. The Ruhar goggles allowed the light of the beacon to shine through, dampening the intensity only a bit. Now the top of the mountain dissolved into a searing, intense thin beam of light lancing up into the frozen gray clouds. Automatically, the goggles protected the eyes of the wearers, and also automatically lifted the protection within less than three seconds.

"Wow!" Ski shouted.

"Hot damn!" Jesse replied, and high-fived Ski's gloved hand.

The Kristang projector they had spent the past eight days excavating, examining and preparing had just fired six low-power shots up into the sky. The test shots were aimed at targets in orbits far from Paradise, in an area clear of ships. Even at super low power, the backscatter from maser photons burning through the clouds would have blinded the two exposed humans. Dave felt a welcome warmth on his face from the still-glowing clouds. "That felt good."

"Stay where you are," Irene warned. "The shockwave will be hitting your position soon." The first test shot had been more powerful than the others, as the first shot had to clear a temporary hole up through the clouds. Now that hole was slamming closed at supersonic speed, and a sound of tremendous, ground-shaking thunder rolled over the frozen landscape. Dave and Jesse lay flat, faces down, as the wind of the shockwave blasted them, grateful for the protection of the ridge they were behind. And grateful the hamster engineers had been successful in reducing the power of the projector's maser beam shots. If the projector had been firing at full power, even from forty miles, the backscatter of the maser beam in the atmosphere could have fried exposed skin. Projectors were designed to punch through the shields of a starship; collateral damage to the surface around them was a very minor consideration.

Jesse stripped off his gloves, helmet and cap, unzipped his parka, and gratefully accepted the hot cup of tomato soup from Shauna. After being outside, the interior of the Buzzard felt like a sauna. It felt good. So did the hot cup in his hands. "Did it work? The test?"

"We won't know until the Ruhar complete their analysis," Derek Bonsu answered from the cockpit, leaning over to speak through the open doorway. "We're supposed to get an update when Major Perkins gets back."

Perkins had been given the honor of observing the test from the Ruhar's command Buzzard, parked a quarter mile away. According to the Ruhar, it was an honor; Perkins was not so happy about it. Most of the Ruhar project team openly resented humans accompanying them, and Perkins had to stretch her patience and tactfulness to the limit when dealing with the hamsters. Fortunately, she was mostly able to pretend their subtle insults did not translate well over zPhones, and she concealed her growing fluency in understanding spoken Ruhar. When Perkins came into the Buzzard, half frozen from the short walk, she gave her team the good news while taking off her parka. "The test was a success, based on preliminary data," Perkins announced, less happily than might have been expected.

"However," Irene rolled her eyes.

"Hmm?" Perkins asked.

"With the Ruhar, there's *always* a 'however', ma'am," Irene observed. "This is the sixth projector we've been involved in reactivating with them, and every time the preliminary data shows the test was successful. And every freakin' time, the hamsters decide they need another round of testing. And that second test always shows everything is great."

"Lieutenant, I understand you are annoyed at how slow the process is going," Perkins said, without sounding as if she was being understanding about it. "You need to keep in mind that the Ruhar are dealing with alien technology, *enemy* technology. They not only have to make certain these projectors won't blow up in their faces, they need to know they can rely on the projector grid for planetary defense. Even a battlegroup being based here doesn't ensure our safety; the Kristang could attack while the battlegroup is deployed somewhere else. That Elder power tap and the comm nodes they found make this planet a prime target. If that means the hamsters are being super picky about the condition of each projector, I am fully on board with that."

"How long, ma'am?" Dave asked.

"If the Ruhar decide they require a second test-"

Trouble on Paradise

"And they will," Shauna groaned.

"-then we will be here another six days, before we can start packing our suitcases."

"Six days?!" Irene slumped in her chair. Six days was bad enough when they were reactivating projectors in a nice climate. Six days of enforced idleness, and six days when she couldn't fly. At least when they were at a site with pleasant weather, they could get out of the cramped Buzzard. They could set up tents for privacy, put up a volleyball net, sit around a campfire in the evenings. In the frigid hell of the arctic on Paradise, the six of them were stuck inside the Buzzard all day. Six people; three women and three men. Living, sleeping, cooking, using the one tiny bathroom. That got old really fast.

The problem wasn't just being stuck inside the Buzzard for six more days, it was six days during which there was absolutely nothing for the humans to do. The Ruhar grudgingly trusted the humans to set up and operate the drill, to give the Ruhar access to the buried projector. Once the drill created an opening in the projector's casing, the Ruhar took over, and did not allow the humans even to visit a projector. The arrogance of the Ruhar was supremely irritating, especially so because Major Perkins' team had reactivated projectors all on their own, without the Ruhar having any idea their planet even contained such a weapon.

"Oh, this sucks!" Jesse squeezed Shauna's hand. "The weather forecast is for blizzard conditions, starting in six days." If the second test was successful, and that was a sure as a sunrise, the Ruhar would want the humans to immediately begin disassembling the drill rig and pack it back into the Buzzard. Although the Ruhar could take their own sweet time inspecting and testing a projector, they demanded the humans to move quickly, with no excuses. High winds, subzero temperatures and heavy snow could not be allowed to delay the operation. That meant the six humans would be stumbling around, half frozen, wrestling the balky drill rig back into the Buzzard. With the back ramp of the Buzzard open, snow would be swirling into the cargo compartment, drifting into every corner and crevice. Irene and Derek would have the heaters on maximum power, worried that extensive cold soaking would cause a critical Buzzard component to fail. Spare parts were a long, long distance away.

"I'm not looking forward to it either, Colter," Perkins said in a matter of fact manner. "This is the job we signed up for. We begged the Ruhar for this assignment; the whole planet is watching us." On behalf of UNEF, Perkins herself had done the begging and groveling to keep humans part of the projector reactivation team.

"Ma'am," Shauna suggested, "there are parts of the rig we can take apart and pack away now. We don't need the components for drilling." Part of the rig scaffolding was in use to give Ruhar technicians and scientists access to the underground projector, but the actual drilling part of the operation was complete.

"You are sure about that, Jarrett?" Major Perkins was skeptical. "We've never done that."

"Yes, ma'am, it's in the drill rig manual," Shauna pulled up a schematic on her tablet. "The hamsters take the drill rig apart sometimes, when they want to replace just part of the system, for field maintenance." On the mission, the humans had not been allowed, or trusted, to take apart the drill rig. Instead, the Ruhar provided a refurbished drill rig after the team had worked on three projectors. "It's easy," she pointed to the schematic. "It's looks easy, anyway. There's a set of videos that walks us through the process. If we take it apart, we can cut the final part of the stowing process to a couple hours."

Perkins looked at the file on her own tablet. It did look simple and easy, and the process did not require anything complicated. Which was good, because the translated Ruhar instructions read something like 'Being Tab A into Slot B, for making joyous assembly'. It reminded Perkins of the Chinese instructions for the washing machine in what used to be her apartment back on Earth. The rig had been designed to break down easily. "We'll look at this. This is good, Jarrett. If it checks out, I'll talk to the Ruhar about it."

"Ma'am? If we're not needed here until the test," Derek inquired, "could we fly someplace else to wait it out? There's a Ruhar base only three hours south of here." While the climate at the base was not tropical, it was warmer than the bone-chilling cold at the projector site. They could go outside without risking frostbite and death. And they could live in the base buildings, rather than being stuck inside the Buzzard the whole time.

"I'll need to consider that." Perkins' instinct was to keep the Buzzard and her crew right where they were. The Ruhar did not need humans to reactivate the remaining projectors on the planet, UNEF through Perkins had begged for the opportunity to participate and demonstrate that humans could be trustworthy and useful. Abandoning the arctic projector site, simply because it was unpleasant, would send a signal that humans were soft. And the Ruhar base mentioned by Derek Bonsu was unlikely to be thrilled with the idea of hosting a group of humans. The base commander might outright refuse permission for humans to land there, even if Perkins offered to set up tents for her team to live in, so the Ruhar didn't have to encounter humans frequently. Despite Perkins and her team having reactivated projectors and blasted a Kristang battlegroup out of the sky, humans overall were still not viewed positively by Ruhar. The Ruhar natives still had hard feelings against humans, who they saw as ignorant, backwards aliens used as a goon squad by the Kristang, to force Ruhar off the world they considered to be their home.

The real mission of Perkins' team was not to drill down into projector sites to allow access for the Ruhar technicians. The mission was public relations, on behalf of all humans on Paradise. "I can sound out the Ruhar team leader here, she may have people who would appreciate a couple days away from," she tried to think of a nice way talk about the frozen hell they were living in, then settled for, "here." The Ruhar team had three Buzzards, and had set up two warm, large prefab shelters for use only by Ruhar. If some of the Ruhar were not needed for the second test, Perkins could use transporting them aboard their Buzzard as an excuse to fly her own team out.

The battered and overworked Kristang frigate *To Seek Glory in Battle is Glorious* drifted through space, eighty million kilometers from the planet known to Kristang as Pradassis. Following the *Glory*'s escape from the deadly trap Admiral Ferlant's Ruhar Fleet squadron had sprung on the Kristang pursuit force, the *Glory* had been badly in need of a major overhaul merely to keep the reactor and life support systems functioning at a minimum level. Instead of including the *Glory* as part of his remaining force, so that little ship could go home with the rest of the Kristang force, Admiral Kekrando had declared that frigate lost with all hands. The admiral had loaded two dropships with critical supplies and spare parts, and sent them on an unmanned one-way trip to the *Glory*, with orders for that ship to perform what repairs the crew could complete on their own. Since then, the *Glory* had been alone in deep space, outside the typical patrol areas of the Kristang guard force. The ship's stealth field was drawn tightly around it; the stealth generator and its support systems had been the first item the crew had repaired as best they could. The sensor field was offline, although that system was in reasonably good condition, by the standards of warrior Kristang. The sensor field was not offline for the purpose of maintenance, it was offline because the *Glory* could not risk its sensor field giving away the fact that an undeclared Kristang ship was lingering in the star system. For the purpose of hiding, using only passive sensors was the ship's best tactic, for the Ruhar guard ships were hammering the area around the planet with powerful active sensor pulses. Even with its passive sensor network half blinded, the *Glory* could easily tell how many enemy ships were searching, and where. Every time an active sensor pulse swept across their ship, even from eighty million kilometers away, the entire crew held their breath and prayed that their creaky stealth field generator would keep limping along for just a few more days, or weeks.

When the crew unpacked the unmanned dropships, they were initially delighted to find that the remnants of Kekrando's battlegroup had donated a generous supply of spare parts for the *Glory*'s jump drive. Unfortunately, in order to conceal the ship's presence, the *Glory* could not jump at all. A jump would create two distinctive gamma ray bursts, at both ends of the jump wormhole; that would be like ringing a bell to announce the *Glory*'s presence. The Ruhar guard force might suspect Kekrando had left behind one or two ships to spy on Ruhar activity, or to create mischief. They did not know for certain that Kekrando had violated the cease fire terms, and to protect Kekrando's force, the *Glory* must remain hidden until after Kekrando's ships had been transported away by Jeraptha star carriers. Only once the Jeraptha ships had jumped away could the *Glory* begin its mission.

To perform its mission, the *Glory* needed to do two things. First, it had not only to hide, but to give the Ruhar no evidence that an undeclared Kristang ship was in the star system. And second, the *Glory* needed to get closer to the planet, without jumping.

"Captain, I do not see how we can accomplish our mission," second officer Smando said quietly while two ship's two senior officers were enjoying their midday meal in the captain's cramped quarters. 'Enjoy' was perhaps not an accurate description, for the *Glory*'s crew had been enraged to discover that among the supplies Admiral Kekrando had sent, the only food was survival rations. The homeward-bound ships of Kekrando's battlegroup had kept the best food for themselves. So Smando and his captain were choking down survival biscuits, soaked in cups of hot but thin chom.

"Specifically?" The Captain asked as he broke off a piece of biscuit to dunk in his cup of chom. The concrete-like biscuit did not actually dissolve or even soften in the chom, but dunking it gave a pleasing illusion that the captain could do something to make his food more palatable.

"Specifically, as we approach Pradassis, we come within the patrol area of the Ruhar guard force. Our engineers have performed miracles to keep the stealth field working. They can't conceal all evidence of our presence here. Sooner or later-"

"Given this ship's service record, I am betting on sooner," the captain mumbled over a mouthful of biscuit.

"Yes, sooner. Those guard force ships are going to detect our reactor exhaust, or the thousand other types of particles we leave in our wake, even when the ship is in perfect condition."

"You joke, Smando," the captain slapped the table. "This ship has never been in perfect condition. Not even the day it left the construction yard."

"True."

"Tell me, Smando, given that it is inevitable the Ruhar guard force will detect the presence of a concealed ship, what would be even better than our continued ability to avoid detection?"

"A critical engineering failure that leaves us unable to perform our mission," Smando spoke words that would be considered treason aboard most other ships; a failure to display the proper warrior attitude at all times. Aboard the *Glory*, the crew had had more than their fill of proper warrior spirit crap, and preferred realism. "So we have to announce ourselves to the Ruhar, and be sent safely home?"

"Hmm. That is better," the captain chuckled. "What I was thinking of was, for the guard force ships to detect evidence of an enemy ship, but not find us."

"I," Smando paused to think. He knew how his captain thought. He ventured a guess. "The absolute best would be for the enemy to be tracking the *Glory*, but not be tracking us?"

"Exactly! Excellent thinking, Smando! The enemy identifies signatures of every ship under Kekrando's command. They know which ships are awaiting a ride home from the insects," he used a disparaging term for the Jeraptha, "and they know which ships were destroyed for certain. The only ship missing from those two lists is the *Glory*."

"And they have our signature in their sensor databases." Smando could not yet guess what his captain was planning. "Our most distinctive signature is our jump drive, but we will not be jumping."

"Correct."

"Then there is our reactor exhaust, although we are operating at minimum power, so," he stopped guessing. "How can we make the enemy think they are tracking this ship, without them actually following our trail?"

The captain attempted another bite of biscuit, before dropping it back to soak in the chom. "In the days when ocean ships had metal hulls, this was after sails and before the use of aluminum and composites," the *Glory*'s captain intoned in a voice that the ship's crew knew meant he was going to talk for a while on an obscure topic. "The poor quality of the primitive steel, and the salt environment, caused the hulls to corrode, so the crews had to constantly scrape off the old paint, and apply new paint to protect the hull. It was a chore the old saltwater sailors hated with a passion."

"Yes," the second officer indulged his commanding officer, wondering whether a poem was about to be composed for the occasion. The captain had a reputation throughout the clan for creating amusing, if not properly warrior-like, poems for all occasions.

"What we need, Smando, is paint scrapers."

"Mmm hmm," the second officer agreed. There was little actual paint aboard the ship, and little need to scrape what little there was. Color was within the materials the ship was composed of, or color could be changed by manipulating nanoparticles with various materials.

"Come," the captain announced, standing up as he placed the remainder of his survival biscuit to soak in the cooling cup of chom. "We will ask the fabrication shop to create several eights of paint scrapers."

"And then?"

"Then," the captain said with the slow, two eye blink that was the Kristang form of a wink, "we will step outside for some fresh air."

As Perkins expected, the meeting with the Ruhar projector team leader did not result in the humans being allowed to fly south for a couple days of R&R in a somewhat warmer climate. Instead, Derek Bonsu's idea to fly south for a couple days had completely backfired on the humans. After the end of the status meeting, during which it had been decided a second test was needed to confirm the projector was fully operational, Perkins approached the Ruhar project leader. "Ma'am, the forecast calls for bad weather closing in. That won't affect your people working down in the projector, but since most personnel aren't needed to prepare for the test, I thought it might be prudent to fly nonessential people out ahead of the weather. We could bring people back in time for the test."

Trouble on Paradise

The project leader had been considering a similar idea in the back of her mind. Perkins mentioning it spurred her into action. "I agree, that would be prudent. Would you want to send some of your team with us?"

Major Emily Perkins was not yet an expert at reading the facial expressions and body language of aliens, even vaguely humanoid aliens like the Ruhar. She was experienced enough to know the Ruhar did not like the idea of humans flying with them. She also knew the question implied that the humans' Buzzard was expected to remain on site. Emily kept her disappointment from showing. "No, ma'am, I think my team needs to remain here, in case there is a problem with the drill rig."

"Very well," the zPhone translated the project leader's actual words. "We will return before the second test, then."

"I've got something," the sensor technician declared quietly. "It's *something*."

"You are certain?" Asked the captain of the Ruhar frigate *Mem Hertall*. His little ship, once part of Commodore Ferlant's force guarding the planet Gehtanu all on their own, had been detailed to sweep the system for hidden Kristang ships. All the ships declared by the Kristang Admiral Kekrando were gathered at the rendezvous point in the outskirts of the star system, waiting for a pair of Jeraptha star carriers to transport them away. What worried Ruhar Fleet Command was the possibility that Kekrando had not declared all his ships. Fleet Command Intelligence suspected there was one, possibly two frigate-sized ships lingering in the system. The *Mem Hertall* and two other frigates had been assigned search areas, and were crisscrossing the star system in a grid search. Finding a small, stealthed ship in the vast gulf of a star system was nearly impossible, so the search force was not looking for ships; they were looking for traces all ships inevitably left behind. Even the stealthiest ship gave off gases from propulsion, from tiny leaks in the hull, from the operation of airlocks and dropship docking bays, even from harsh solar radiation baking off a ship's outer coating. Ships had to radiate waste heat intermittently. The powerful magnetic fields of their reactor containments systems disturbed particles of the solar wind as the ship passed through, leaving a swirling and electrically-charged wake behind the ship. No ship could pass through space, or even remain motionless in space, without leaving *some* sort of residual trace.

When the planet Gehtanu became important enough, the star system would be saturated with satellites creating multiple, overlapping stealth detection grids. That day would be a long time in the future; the Ruhar had not yet even installed a strategic defense satellite network around Gehtanu. Until detection grids were online, the Ruhar had to rely on ships slowly and painstakingly scanning the star system, their sensor fields set to maximum coverage. In such long search missions, the critical factor limiting the effectiveness of the ships was not their fuel, or food stores or the condition of critical components that needed maintenance. The critical factor was the boredom level of the crew. That is why the *Mem Hertall*'s captain wished to make certain the sensor technician was not merely seeing what he very much wanted to see in the data: evidence of an enemy ship. The possibility of action, and an end to a long and tedious patrol assignment. And the hope of the crew being given a well-deserved and long overdue shore leave on Gehtanu.

"Captain," the sensor tech announced with confidence, "I know this is a trail left by a ship, and I even know which ship it is."

The captain raised his chin and tilted his head back, in the Ruhar gesture to express surprise or skepticism; the equivalent of a raised eyebrow. Ruhar could move their eyebrows, but they usually used their chins instead. "Explain. Show me the data."

"See the rhodium signature?" The technician pointed to the display. "Typical hull coating for Kristang ships. Molecules have been ablating off as the ship passes through charged particles of the solar wind; they can't activate shields in full, because they know we would eventually detect that power radiation."

"Agreed."

"So, this cloud we found was left behind by a Kristang ship. Now, see this line for palladium? Also lanthanum. This particular ship's hull coating has been patched, poorly patched by whatever they had available at the time. And *this* ship has a distinctive ratio of rhodium to palladium and lanthanum. I recognize this ship; it's in our database. This is our old friend the *Glory*," she patted the display almost with affection.

The captain was still skeptical. "You are that certain?"

"Absolutely," the tech declared with utter confidence. The Kristang frigate *To Seek Glory in Battle is Glorious* had been in multiple combat actions around Gehtanu, and during those engagements the *Glory*'s hull had been bathed by maserlight. Ships in combat were protected by energy shields that bent maser or particle beams safely around a ship's hull, or dispersed the intense hair-thin beams. Some of the energy of the incoming beam bled through the shield, to be scattered across the surface of the hull. Even with the beam attenuated, enough energy remained to cook the ship's hull, and flake off tiny pieces of the hull coating. Those drifting particles, remnants of the battle, had been scooped up and analyzed by Commodore Ferlant's ships, adding the distinctive chemical signature of that ship to the Fleet database as the *Glory*. "No question about it. The Fleet database identified this chemical trail as the *Glory* with a hundred percent confidence. The *Glory* was overdue for major maintenance when she arrived in this system, and she has been limping along with the Kristang's signature half-assed repairs since then. Her reactor leaks; the trail she leaves in her wake includes helium-3, both raw and irradiated. There is also a measurable amount of free oxygen behind her; she must have a hull breach somewhere that they didn't quite fix properly."

"That ship was declared lost due to battle damage, by Admiral Kekrando," The captain mused.

"True," the tech smiled. "This would be the first time we were lied to by the Kristang?"

The captain smiled and shook his head. "If the Kristang ever tell us the truth, *that* will be a first. Very well, we will pursue this lead. Good job. I will be counting on you not to lose track of our quarry." If a Kristang frigate was in the Gehtanu system without declaring its presence, it was in direct violation of the admittedly humiliating ceasefire terms agreed to by Admiral Kekrando. Therefore, the *Mem Hertall* and her sister ships would be within the rules of engagement to shoot first and ask questions never. Captain Rastall had four missiles loaded and ready in their launch tubes, awaiting only a target and launch authorization. One forward and one aft maser turret was energized at all times, with the turrets being rotated as the active units had to be taken down for maintenance. Rastall was determined to kill whatever ship was lurking out there, because any hidden Kristang ship was most assuredly hostile. Once Admiral Kekrando's ships departed aboard Jeraptha star carriers, there would be little to prevent a 'rogue' Kristang ship from attacking Gehtanu. Ruhar ships could pursue and destroy the attacker, or attackers, and lodge a completely useless protest through diplomatic channels. If the attack was sufficiently brutal, it might attract the notice of the Jeraptha. The Jeraptha might even authorize a retaliation; in extreme cases the Jeraptha themselves had hit the Kristang to teach them a lesson. All of those potential actions would be of no comfort to dead Ruhar on Gehtanu. Rastall returned to his command chair, and ordered his ship to change course, to follow the faint chemical trail. "Signal the *Toman* and *Grathur* our intentions," he referred to the pair of frigates helping the *Hertall* to search the star system.

"What are our intentions, Captain?" The executive office asked with a knowing smile.

"I intend to find, and destroy, an annoyingly persistent enemy ship that has survived far too long already."

"This still sucks," Dave commented as he spooned vegetable soup into his mouth. "I mean, yeah, it could be worse, but it does still suck."

"How bad does it suck, Ski?" Jesse knew the answer, he also knew his friend needed to vent.

"Before, if we'd all been stuck in the Buzzard six more days, that would have sucked a bowling ball through fifty feet of garden hose," Dave declared.

"And now?"

"Now," Dave contemplated the situation. "Maybe a baseball. Yeah. Same garden hose."

"If the bowling ball had already gone through the hose and stretched it out, it would be easy to get a baseball through there," Jesse pointed out helpfully.

"You're right," Dave said, his expression brightening.

"Oh my God," Shauna said with disgust. "Is this what guys talk about when we're not around?"

"What he meant," Dave came to Jesse's rescue, "is that if we had been stuck in the Buzzard first, this would seem great."

Jesse nodded, not sure whether he should contradict Shauna. Unlike the vast majority of human men on Paradise, he had a semi-girlfriend. No way was he going to do anything to risk that, he was on the edge already.

"We do talk about stupid stuff all the time," Jesse hastened to add. "That was a Nobel prize-winning conversation, compared to most of the stuff we talk about."

"I can believe it," Shauna agreed. She shook another pinch of hot pepper powder into her vegetable soup. It was the third day in a row they ate rehydrated vegetable soup for lunch, and they were all getting tired of it. "You're right, Dave, this does suck."

Somehow, humans had gotten screwed on the whole deal. Most of the Ruhar had bugged out of the arctic base, leaving only one of their three Buzzards and five hamsters to prepare for the second test. As a gesture of goodwill, the Ruhar had left one of their portable shelters for the humans to live in, so they weren't all crammed together in the Buzzard. Irene and Derek declined the offer to live in the shelter, saying they wanted more time in the Buzzard to use it as a simulator for flight training. Shauna thought her friend Irene was doing more than 'simulating' certain intimate activities with their cute copilot Derek, but so far Irene hadn't said anything to Shauna about it.

The worst part of the deal was that, at the end of the projector test, the humans would be expected to take down and pack away not only their own shelter, but also the shelter being used by the Ruhar technical team. The weather shortly after the test would be a full-blown blizzard, and the Ruhar would be sure to blame the humans if either of the shelters were damaged in the process of taking them down and stowing them in the Ruhar's Buzzard. After securing the shelters, Perkins and her team would need to finish stowing away the drill rig. What should have been a matter of two or three uncomfortable hours was now looking like it would take a full day, or more. The humans would be working outside in the cold, freezing fingers while the Ruhar sat inside their warm, cozy Buzzard's passenger cabin, eating snacks and taking naps. Any delay would give the Ruhar one more reason to remove humans from any meaningful assignments on Paradise. That was the deal the team had signed up for; humans did the crappy grunt work, and they were expected to smile and keep their mouths shut about it. Shauna picked up a slice of potato with her spoon. "Dave, do you still think this is better than farming?"

"Oh, *hell* yes," Jesse answered on behalf of Dave, who nodded vigorously. "Way better."

CHAPTER FOUR

Baturnah Logellia came directly from a very uncomfortable Ruhar-only meeting, to her regular weekly meeting with the UNEF chief of intelligence. She was dreading what was going to be a very, very uncomfortable conversation. "Good morning, General Marcellus," she said as she walked into her office and sat down heavily in her chair.

"Good morning, Administrator Logellia."

"General, we're going to skip the usual briefing today. Something has come up; your headquarters will be officially informed soon, I want to tell you personally."

Marcellus kept himself from showing the exasperation he felt inwardly. For a brief time, things had been going reasonably well for UNEF, now that the Ruhar fleet had stationed a battlegroup at Paradise. Marcellus had been waiting for the spell to be broken, for disaster to strike UNEF again. Was this it? "I am listening."

"These Keepers of the Faith among your people have created a very serious problem for both of us," Baturnah explained. "They actively assisted the Kristang during the projector crisis. They rejected UNEF's declaration of loyalty to the Ruhar coalition. Now thousands of them have volunteered to leave this planet with the Kristang. You can understand that these developments have made my people question whether we could ever trust humans."

The Jeraptha were sending star carriers to transport the survivors of Admiral Kekrando's battlegroup, and his ground troops, away from the Paradise system. That the Kristang had offered to take their human allies with them when their remaining forces left Paradise had surprised both Ruhar and humans; UNEF and the Keepers. That any human would volunteer to leave Paradise with the Kristang had also been surprising to UNEF. That so far, five thousand Keepers would be leaving had astonished UNEF HQ and alarmed the Ruhar. "These 'Keepers' have left official military service, we can't prevent them from going with the Kristang if they choose to do that."

"Yes, you could."

"Excuse me?" Marcellus asked, confused. "We could what?"

"Stop these Keepers from leaving with the Kristang. You could do it; you have chosen not to. Even though you surely know the Keepers are making a horrible, foolish mistake. Humans who leave this planet with the Kristang will almost certainly be killed; either to punish humans in general, or for sport. The Kristang are absolutely not acting for the benefit of humans."

"The Keepers are adults, they are capable of making their own decisions, even if our leadership strongly believes the Kristang are likely leading them to their deaths. It is not our way to force people to act against their personal beliefs," Marcellus explained. What he did not say was there had been much debate on that subject at UNEF HQ, with many, including Marcellus, arguing they should indeed forcibly prevent the Keepers from going with the Kristang. The debate had been heated, and ultimately, the decision had been made that UNEF would not interfere with the Keepers who wanted to join the Kristang. UNEF did demand those Keepers remove UNEF and other military insignia from their clothing, which had become a sticky situation. The Keepers were happy to remove UNEF insignia, but refused to surrender their national military symbols, or rank insignia. It was UNEF, the Keepers declared, that were the traitors. In their minds, the Keepers the only ones continuing the mission they had been assigned by lawful national authorities on Earth, so only Keepers had a right to wear military insignia. For now, UNEF HQ had decided not to contest the issue with force.

"Yes, that is one possible reason," Baturnah cocked her head in an eerily humanlike gesture. "Your leadership may also be thinking you are better off without the most fanatical of Keepers causing problems here on Gehtanu. Having them voluntarily leave the planet solves a lot of problems for you."

Marcellus smiled with one side of his mouth. "You might be correct about that, I can't speak for all of UNEF leadership."

"What worries me deeply is I do not understand their motivation; it is extremely puzzling."

How to explain human motivations to an alien, Marcellus asked himself? He wasn't sure he fully understood the motivations of the Keepers, because to Marcellus, they were stubborn idiots who refused to accept the truth. "Each person has their own set of motivations for choosing to leave with the Kristang. Many of the Keepers-"

"General Marcellus, I believe we have experienced a miscommunication," the Burgermeister said slowly, taking care to pronounce each word with as little squeak in her voice as she could manage. She checked her zPhone to assure it was translating correctly. "When I said 'their', I was referring to the *Kristang*, not to humans who are choosing to leave Gehtanu. These humans, as you said, each have their own reasons. It is difficult to accept that your people were lured away from Earth to serve a species you now know to be your enemy. I believe these 'Keepers' are unwilling, or unable, to accept the harsh reality of their situation."

"Oh. I understand now," Marcellus nodded, smiling, although he did not like the alien's judgement on humans the Ruhar could not possibly understand.

"Good," Administrator Logellia returned the smile, showing her substantial front teeth. "What I do not understand is why the Kristang are bothering to bringing the Keepers with them? Over five thousand humans have volunteered to go offworld with the Kristang, and the numbers are increasing as the evacuation day approaches," she observed. Would those numbers decline as Kristang transport ships arrived in orbit, and reality of leaving Gehtanu and UNEF set in? The Ruhar government, and UNEF, were eager to see what would happen. The Ruhar military was concerned the Keepers going offworld might someday present a security risk although no one could imagine how that might happen. "That many humans, *aliens*, presents a substantial logistics burden on the Kristang. They will need to provide human food, at least until they arrive at their destination and the Keepers are able to grow their own food."

"Maybe the Kristang are planning to bring the Keepers to a planet where the native life is compatible with human nutrition needs?" Marcellus was guessing, and guessing on the hopeful side of the unknown. The idea that the Kristang were bringing Keepers offworld only to kill them was too depressing to contemplate.

Baturnah lifted one shoulder in the Ruhar equivalent of a shrug. "The Kristang have refused to say what their plans are for the Keepers. We inquired, and were told that under the cease-fire terms, the Kristang have no obligation to reveal their plans or destination for after the Jeraptha star carriers rendezvous with the Thuranin." She frowned toward Marcellus. "Legally, they are within their rights. What the Kristang plan to do with your Keepers is not our concern, although I fear for their fate. My question is what the Kristang hope to gain by bringing your Keepers with them. In my opinion, it would be better for the Kristang to leave your malcontents," she paused to check whether that word translated correctly, "here to create problems for UNEF and my government. The only reason I can think of to motivate the Kristang would be for them to sow discontent within UNEF, but," she held up her hands.

"Yes, why would they bother?" Marcellus mused. "They are leaving this planet, and UNEF is, I have to admit, of no military importance."

"I am pleased that we agree," Baturnah said with another toothy grin. "The reason I mention the Keepers is they have caused considerable anxiety within my government, and some decisions have been made at the Federal level that I do not fully agree with. As you know, the population of Gehtanu is increasing, there are transport ships arriving every month. My people are moving back into villages that were evacuated during the, well, we do not need to mention that unhappy time," she frowned. What she meant was when UNEF had been enforcing the Kristang's evacuation of the planet. "What matters to you is many of my people have expressed interest in residing on the continent you call Lemuria."

"Lemuria. In territory you gave to UNEF?" Marcellus asked, alarmed.

"Unfortunately, yes. The communication that will be officially delivered to your headquarters today states that your people will be relocated to southern Lemuria, across the mountain range. The area we have selected is not a jungle like where you are living now; this new area had a climate more like Georgia in your United States."

Marcellus did not immediately reply, while he considered the implications. Southern Lemuria was in many ways greatly preferable to the steaming jungles where UNEF was now living. Many Earth crops did not grow well in the jungle, and daytime temperatures could be uncomfortably hot. If the Ruhar had given UNEF the choice between being near the equator, or in southern Lemuria, UNEF would not have chosen the jungle. The only reason UNEF had been moved to the jungle was it was closer to the northern continent, reducing transport time and effort for the Ruhar. But now, when UNEF personnel had expended enormous time and effort to clear land, plant crops and construct villages, it would be a bitter pill for the humans to be forcibly relocated and start over. "Is this issue open to negotiation?" Marcellus asked fearfully.

"No," she shook her head. "Many of my people feel that your current location is too close to our population centers, and to critical infrastructure such as the cargo Launcher. Also, there are commercial interests among my people who wish to develop the northern seacoast of Lemuria. Having humans in close proximity would not be good for," she did the one shoulder shrug, "property values. I am sorry that commercial concerns affect relations between our peoples, but please understand that maintaining a battlegroup at Gehtanu requires not only an ongoing search for Elder artifacts, it requires a substantial and growing population. To encourage people to move to Gehtanu, we must offer business opportunities. The battlegroup protects your people as much as my own, so encouraging development is to the benefit of UNEF."

"I understand." Real estate? UNEF was being relocated, again, because of a real estate deal? Marcellus reflected ruefully that in this regard, the Ruhar were no different from the humans they deemed primitive. "Administrator Logellia, I feel I must point out that after the Keepers leave with the Kristang, the overwhelming majority of UNEF forces will be people who have formally declared loyalty to the Ruhar. I also remind you that Major Perkins' team rescued this planet from the Kristang by destroying a battlegroup."

Baturnah nodded slowly. "We appreciate what Major Perkins and her team did. And we understand the importance of UNEF's pledge of loyalty. General, there simply is not enough trust of humans within my people. This relocation will be inconvenient; however, it may actually be for the best in the long term. Having our peoples physically separated will allow tensions to cool, and it will remove the possibility of incidents that could further damage relations. Over time, my people may come to view humans as farmers who happen to live on part of our planet, rather than occupiers who have been conquered."

Marcellus hoped the harsh words of her last sentence was a function of the zPhone translator. The Ruhar would be happy for humans to be living quietly in far southern Lemuria, until the Ruhar population increased, and the aliens decide they needed *lebensraum*. What would happen to the defenseless humans then? "Thank you, Administrator." He stood and made a short bow toward her. "I will convey your concerns to my leadership." As he was escorted out of the building, he thought to himself that it was good he hadn't put any effort into replacing the tent he lived in with a real hut.

Major Emily Perkins was escorted across the airfield by a Ruhar guard. A smiling, friendly Ruhar guard who kept his sidearm in an unobtrusive holster. Still, Perkins had an armed guard escorting her everywhere she went on the Ruhar airbase. She was allowed access to the military base. But she was neither trusted nor particularly welcome. As they walked toward the administration building, Perkins saw Ruhar giving her unfriendly looks, and one gave her a rude gesture using crossed fingers lifted in her direction. Perkins looked straight ahead, a ghost of a smile on her lips. Be friendly, she reminded herself. Don't provoke anything. We just came back from a miserable mission in the frigid arctic, where we helped reactivate maser projectors that will protect this planet. If all the Ruhar on the airbase knew about that, would they be more welcoming?

Probably not. Humans on Paradise were still viewed as an occupying force; primitive lackeys of the hated Kristang. The fact that the local government allowed Perkins' team to fly around like leashed pets was not going to change the minds of the native Ruhar.

And while she was thinking of humans on Paradise, she saw across the airfield a group of humans being marched off a giant Dumbo transport aircraft. Even at a distance, she could tell by their dress uniforms the humans were UNEF officers. "Excuse me," she asked her escort through the zPhone translator, "who are those humans?" Perkins still had a good pipeline to UNEF HQ, and she was not aware of any high-level meeting scheduled for that day.

"Those?" her escort grimaced, using the exact same facial contortions as a human. "They are, you call them Those Who Keep the Faith?" The Ruhar's translated voice stumbled.

"Oh," it was Emily's turn to grimace. "Keepers. We call them Keepers. Actually," she smiled and winked, knowing the Ruhar used the same facial expressions, "they call themselves Keepers. *We* have less polite names for those idiots."

"Uh? Ha, ha!"

"On Earth, we have a large bird that does not fly," Perkins struggled with how to describe an ostrich. "When it is faced with a predator, it will bury its head in the sand rather than confront the danger." She knew that was a myth, but it made a good point for her story. "Those Keepers can't deal with the fact that we got suckered by the Kristang, so they cling to their original mission orders."

The escort was silent, puzzled by the translation. He pressed a button to replay and listened again. "Major Perkins, I am curious. The strategy you described is not wise for the survival of the bird that is unable to fly. Would not such a bird quickly have gone extinct?"

Perkins had to stop herself from rolling her eyes. He had completely missed the point of her story. "Oh, for crying out- what I meant is-"

"Or," the escort's face lit up as he had a thought, "is there another factor you did not mention? Does the head of this bird emit heat, and the predators on your planet use infrared vision? In that case, such a survival strategy would be quite successful!

Although," he paused to touch a finger to his lips, "how would the bird know whether the predator has left the area?"

"Oh, I, forget it. I will explain later." She was relieved that they had reached the door of the administration building, and the escort needed to go in first.

Perkins' meeting was with the Ruhar woman she still thought of as 'The Burgermeister'; Deputy Administrator Baturnah Logellia. Recent rumors had Logellia soon moving up to Chief Administrator; the current chief was long known to have desired a move back to his home planet. Perkins had developed a very good working relationship with Logellia, and considered that relationship to be one of UNEF's greatest assets on Paradise. The Deputy Administrator was waiting in her office, her focus on the display in front of her. As soon as Perkins was ushered into the office, Logellia flipped the display closed, rose from her chair and offered a warm handshake. Perkins could still not decide if Logellia genuinely liked humans, or thought of Perkins' team as her pets.

"Major Perkins, did you enjoy your refreshing vacation in the snow? I am sorry there was no opportunity for your team to ski while you were there," she added with a twinkle in her eyes.

"It was delightful, thank you," Perkins winked back. "I highly recommend the experience, to anyone who enjoys frostbite, soul-crushing depression and boredom."

The Burgermeister nodded. "We do appreciate your team's work." She tapped the tablet on her desk. "The report from the mission leader praised the skill and professionalism of your team highly; please convey our regards to them for us."

"I will," Perkins was mildly surprised to hear the Ruhar mission leader had praised her team. In meetings with Perkins, the Ruhar mission leader had treated humans as small and not very bright children. "I am proud of my team's efforts. We are ready for our next mission."

Baturnah plunged ahead, figuring it was best to deliver the bad news right away. "There is, please forgive me if I use the expression incorrectly, good news and bad news on that issue?"

"That is the correct expression," Perkins responded warily. "Traditionally, the bad news is given first."

"Ah, I understand. That way, the good news coming later takes away the sting of the bad news?"

"That is the idea, yes."

"The bad news, then, is there is much pressure coming from the battlegroup commander, to shut down the activities of your team. The commander is concerned about the operational security risks of including aliens in the process of establishing the projector network."

"My team has been restricted to drilling," Perkins protested. "All we do is provide access to the projector control center, we do not descend below the surface at all."

"That is true-"

"That is despite the fact that my team reactivated projectors all by ourselves, and rescued this planet from a Kristang battlegroup. You don't need us to reactivate projectors. *We* don't need *you* to reactivate projectors." Perkins knew she risked insulting the Deputy Administrator; she judged that risk worthwhile, to remind the Ruhar government who had destroyed a Kristang battlegroup that had been hanging over their heads.

"Major," Logellia responded with a quick smile. "Admiral Mohvalu knows your team performed exceptionally. He also knows that your team acted without the permission, or knowledge, of our government. You were beyond our control, and admirals do not like anything to be beyond their command and control."

"We are operating under your control now," Perkins said defensively.

Logellia continued as if Perkins had not spoken. "Admiral Mohvalu expressed to me his concern that when you were working on your own, your team was acting in the interests of humans. Helping us was only a byproduct of your goal of preventing UNEF from falling under the control of the Kristang."

"That is true," Perkins kept her voice cool. "It is also true that allies often find areas of mutual interest. And we were acting under the direction of a Mysterious Benefactor, who I suspected was a group of local Ruhar."

"I personally suspect your 'Emby' was a rival group of Kristang, but our intelligence agencies do not agree." The Ruhar intelligence agencies were still intensely searching for the true identity of 'Emby' and to date they had not a single clue, which made each intelligence agency suspect that 'Emby' was working for another agency. Essentially, the intel agencies were all unhelpfully chasing their tails.

Perkins nodded silently. After the Kristang battlegroup commander essentially surrendered, Perkins and her team had been interrogated for days by Ruhar. The interrogation had not been rough, but it had not been friendly either. Most of the questions had focused on who their Mysterious Benefactor was, a subject about which Perkins and her team had nothing but wild guesses. Based on the questions of her Ruhar interrogators, Perkins thought the Ruhar also had absolutely no idea of Emby's true identity. And they might never know, which was fine with Emily Perkins. Having a Mysterious Benefactor was an ace in the hole, if Perkins was ever able to work with them, or him, or her, again.

Baturnah continued. "When my government, the Federal government, first learned about Admiral Kekrando's battlegroup being destroyed, they were very unhappy. Because the Federal government did *not* want Gehtanu! They wanted to trade this planet for something more valuable; something easier and cheaper to defend. It was only later, when we found that Elder power tap, that the Federal government decided we should keep Gehtanu for ourselves. The federal government does not consider that you did any favors for us, so we do not owe you anything in return."

"We have not asked for favors," Perkins responded in what she hoped was an even tone. "We are working to provide security for this planet, under your control."

"You are now, as you said, acting under our orders. However, if you decide that we are doing something which is not favorable to humans, you might decide to do something that acts against the interests of my people." She paused as a very large dropship revved up its engines and accelerated down the runway, rumbling faster and faster. That type of dropship was called a 'Whale' by the humans, the name referred to a very large aquatic mammal that lived in the oceans on the human's home planet. Unlike the derisive names of 'Buzzard', 'Chicken' or 'Vulture' humans gave to Ruhar combat aircraft, Baturnah had been told 'Whale' was a sign of respect for the gigantic dropship. The office complex buildings had vibration-cancelling technology embedded in floors, walls and ceilings; still Baturnah could feel her desk trembling faintly under her fingertips, so she waited until the noise from the dropship faded.

Perkins did not like the direction the conversation had taken. "UNEF has pledged loyalty to the Ruhar. This was done in our self-interest, as you said, but also because we have come to believe the Kristang are our true enemy. On that issue, our interests are perfectly aligned." The conversation could uselessly go back and forth forever; the Ruhar might never fully trust humans. "Administrator, the bad news is that Admiral Mohvalu wants to terminate my team's participation in the projector missions? You said you also had good news?"

"I do have good news, or news I think is good. I have been able to persuade the Chief Administrator to allow your team to be assigned one last mission. Last, because there are few projectors remaining to be activated. Your team might be assigned other missions in the future, however, this will likely be your last involving the projector network."

"Let me guess," Perkins said with a wry smile, "we are going to the south pole this time." Why not, she thought? Humans would only be assigned to missions the Ruhar did not want.

"No," Baturnah winked. "I have arranged an all-inclusive tropical vacation for you and your team."

"Seriously?" Perkins didn't know if the other woman were joking.

"Seriously. Your people call our planet 'Paradise'. I think this area of Gehtanu is as close to a tropical paradise as you will find on our fair planet. Here," Baturnah opened her display and turned it so Perkins could see. It was a map of the far side of Paradise. Much of one hemisphere was an ocean substantially larger than the Pacific on Earth. That hemisphere held chains of islands, some large and some small. Baturnah zoomed the display on a tiny dot south of the equator. "To be a fully effective mechanism for planetary defense, the projector network must provide overlapping coverage of the entire sky. Because so much of Gehtanu's surface is ocean, the Kristang had to install projectors on some rather small and isolated islands. This is one. To perform this mission, your team pilots will need training to fly a special, long-range version of the aircraft you call a 'Buzzard'. Also, they will need to qualify to perform inflight refueling."

"That will not be a problem," Perkins declared. She had complete confidence in her two pilots.

"You are certain?" Baturnah asked, wary the human commander may be boasting.

"Lt. Striebich performed a precision hover while lowering a drill rig, without any training. Lt. Bonsu was trusted by your own air command to fly a Dobreh gunship."

"True. Will you accept this assignment?"

"Yes," Perkins said without hesitation. "I have only one question. If we perform well, will that help to change your government's mind about resettling UNEF in southern Lemuria?"

"Unfortunately, no."

"But if we perform poorly, that will reflect badly on all humans?"

"Yes, also unfortunately," Baturnah confirmed.

Shit, Perkins said to herself. The only thing worse would be for humans to be excluded from the mission, voluntarily or through a Ruhar ban on human participation. "Thank you for your honesty."

Baturnah gave back a sad smile. "I regret to add that the Ruhar commander of this mission strongly objected to humans being involved. You will need to be, as you say, on your toes. Still," she zoomed the display in farther, so the island could be seen as a lush green dot, fringed by a white beach, in a dazzlingly blue ocean. "At least being on this tropical island will be pleasant for your team?"

"Compared to our last mission, this should be a vacation."

"Good! Major Perkins, I have a favor to request of you. It will benefit you, so I hope you will agree."

Perkins wondered with alarm what the request could be. "What is this favor?"

"I have been trying to arrange a liaison officer for your team; someone to work directly with you, and act as a buffer between yourself and the mission commander. It has been difficult to find someone to act as liaison; it is not a popular assignment. What I have arranged is for one of my nephews- Nephew? Did that translate correctly? My brother's son."

"Nephew is the correct term."

"Good. My nephew is a cadet attending a military academy, he is in his first year, and is here on leave. He is thirteen of your years old?"

Oh, great, Perkins thought. Fantastic. We're going to be babysitters. She smiled as broadly as she could manage. "Administrator, we would be very pleased for your nephew to join my team. I have one question. While he is with us, he will be under my command?"

"That can be arranged," Baturnah nodded. "Thank you, Major. My nephew is very eager for this assignment. I must," she smiled quickly, "tell you, my nephew is young, and even for his age, he is considered somewhat socially awkward. Please do not take offense if he says the wrong thing; he means well."

Doubly great, Perkins groaned inside. "I am sure he will be a great asset to my team." What else could she say?

While Major Perkins was meeting with the Burgermeister, and Irene and Derek were trying to get replacement parts for their Buzzard, Jesse, Dave and Shauna were cleaning their well-used aircraft. They had been flying and living in the Buzzard for weeks, and even the three men agreed the cabin of their ship was getting funky. Jesse and Dave were carrying bags of trash across the landing pad to a dumpster behind a hangar, when Dave saw something that stopped him in his tracks. "Holy crap, dude, check it out," Dave nudged Jesse, pointing toward a hangar a few rows past where their Buzzard was parked.

"What? I- damn! What the hell is *he* doing here?" Jesse exclaimed.

"The Major did say the hamsters had brought in Sleepers for a briefing or something, before they leave the planet. Errant Eric," he used their derisive name for Eric Koblenz, "must be one of them, right?"

"There's nothing right about him, amigo," Jesse muttered. "Something's wrong about him in the head."

"You can say that about all those Sleepers," Dave spat on the tarmac, or whatever material the Ruhar used for the parking aprons and runways at the airbase. "Hey, Jesse, let's ditch this trash and go talk to him."

"Why?" Jesse snorted. "So he can tell us we're traitors? That would be a waste of time. Besides, if he calls me a traitor to my face again, I might have to punch him in his face, and Major Perkins told us to stay out of trouble." Jesse was sure any of the Keepers would love an opportunity to get Jesse or Dave in trouble with their Ruhar hosts.

"Look, the guy is a certified asshole," Dave agreed, "but you think he really wants to go offworld with the lizards? His problem is he's stupid, and he listens to people he should stay away from."

"You're serious?" Jesse asked, fairly astonished.

"Yeah, man. It will be our good deed for the day."

"Good deed for the freakin' year, you mean. And we already destroyed a Kristang battlegroup, I don't need any more good deeds on my record, thank y'all every much," Jesse declared, but Dave could tell he was hesitating.

"Right. You in?"

"You promise to hold me back if I get the urge to punch him?"

"You promise the same for me?"

Trouble on Paradise

"Oh, hell," Jesse sighed. "Ok, let's do it. No need to punch him anyways, the freakin' lizards are sure to get his ass killed up there, if they don't kill him themselves."

They dumped the trash and hurried toward where Eric Koblenz was standing awkwardly in the midst of what Jesse guessed was a hundred Keepers. "Ski, wait," he grabbed Dave's arm. "You really want to persuade this asshole not to throw his life away?"

"Somebody should," Dave nodded.

"In that case, I reckon talking to him is a waste of time. He ain't gonna listen to us, we're traitors, remember? Even if he agrees with us, he'll still go offworld out of stupid pride."

"Yeah, so? You got a better idea?"

"I do." Jesse held up his zPhone, and selected a photo. "See that officer? With the bandages on his face and the arm splint? I think that's Captain Chisolm. He's the only survivor of the raid on that projector site the Ruhar were digging up in Lemuria."

"Shit, that's him?" Dave gaped, and looked between Jesse's zPhone and the officer. "I think you're right, it is him." Major Perkins' team had heard about the failed raid, in which the six Kristang and fifty human attackers had been killed or wounded, with the only survivor being Captain Chisolm. At the time, Perkins and her team had been rather busy flying around reactivating projector sites under the direction of Emby, so they hadn't paid much attention to the incident.

They approached the Ruhar guards around Chisolm and requested permission to speak with their fellow human. One of the Ruhar guards recognized Dave and Jesse, and must have been grateful for their having destroyed a Kristang battlegroup, because she waved them forward. "Speak quickly," she advised. "He will be leaving soon."

"Captain Chisolm?" Dave asked as he gave a salute. "Sir, could we speak with you?"

The Captain returned the salute awkwardly, his right arm was not broken but he had enough tissue damage in the shoulder joint that raising that arm was painful. "Specialist," he began saying to Dave, then turned his attention to Jesse, who had not saluted. "You don't recognize the uniform, soldier?" He asked harshly.

Jesse tapped the UNEF patch on his own uniform. "You're the one who left the service."

Chisolm's jaw set angrily. "The United States Army made me a captain, Specialist. UNEF HQ betrayed our assigned mission, I didn't."

Jesse leaned forward into Chisolm's face. "You think-"

Dave put a hand on Jesse's chest and gently pushed him back. "Don't antagonize the man, Jesse. We need his help."

"Help?" Chisolm was taken aback. "You want to join us?" He asked skeptically.

"No, Sir," Dave explained. "We want to ask your help with-"

"You're not- I know you two!" Recognition dawned on Chisolm's face. "You're on Major Perkins' team," he almost gasped with shock. "You destroyed a battlegroup of our allies, and you are asking *me* for help?"

"The lizards are not our allies," Jesse protested.

"Colter," Chisolm peered at the nametag on Jesse's uniform. "If you came here to argue with me, this is going to be a short conversation."

"No, Sir," Dave assured the Keeper officer. "Jesse, shut up and let me talk."

Before Dave could continue, Chisolm grimaced as he shifted his left arm, the sling was causing pain and no matter how many times he adjusted it, the arm throbbed after a minute. "The two of you assume all of us Keepers are stupid, or we're weak. That we either don't see the truth about the Kristang, or we can't face the truth so we cling to a comforting lie. Is that about it?"

"Sounds about right to me, how about you, Ski?" Jesse replied, arms across his chest.

"I said *not* to antagonize him, Cornpone." Dave pleaded. "Captain, we have different ideas about what we should be doing out here, now that we've lost contact with Earth. You have your opinion, and we have-"

"Opinion?" Chisolm shook his head in a dismissive gesture. "This is not a mere matter of *opinion*, Czajka. The difference between you and me," Chisolm looked at the Keepers standing under the shade of the hangar. "Between you and us, is you believe those 'Fortune Cookies' are real. Right? You think the info we found written into food packaging came from Earth. You think those messages are the straight truth from Earth, and that the Kristang back home have conquered our home planet and are abusing humanity."

"Yeah, so?" Jesse still had his arms firmly across his chest. "Only an idiot would-"

"We believe them, Sir." Dave interrupted, pleading with his eyes for Jesse to shut the hell up.

"The difference is, I don't," Chisolm said with conviction. "*We* don't. The Kristang rescued our planet. The Ruhar attacked us, not the Kristang. We believe those 'Fortune Cookies' are disinformation planted by the Ruhar, to drive a wedge between us and the Kristang, and to sow dissension in the ranks of UNEF." He laughed bitterly. "And it worked, didn't it?"

"How the hell could the Ruhar have planted messages inside food packages that came from Earth, aboard Kristang starships?" Jesse asked in a taunting tone.

"I don't know, but the hamsters have technology beyond our comprehension. Can you say for certain, with *absolute* certainty, that the Ruhar could not have done it?"

Jesse's defiant expression belied his uncertainty. "You can't prove something *didn't* happen. It makes no sense."

"My point, soldier," Chisolm said calmly, "is the difference between UNEF and us Keepers of the Faith isn't stubbornness or stupidity. It's a matter of judgment. Tell me, what would you do if you thought the Fortune Cookies were fakes, planted by the hamsters?" He addressed the question to Dave rather than Jesse.

"Uh, then, shit, Sir. I guess I'd be one of you?" Dave did not like the turn the conversation had taken. Was the difference between UNEF and Keepers really only a matter of judgment, of whether to trust the Ruhar more than the Kristang? Was he the one stubbornly clinging to the UNEF chain of command, rather than thinking for himself?

"But we don't believe that. I mean," Jesse shook his head, angry at Chisolm for trying to confuse him. "We do believe the Fortune Cookies are honest-to-God messages from Earth."

"Yeah, Jesse, but he's right," Dave said hesitantly. "What, hell, what if we found out the hamsters faked the whole thing?"

"Oh, fuck. I've had my mind blown too many times already. You're on his side now, Ski?" Jesse asked, hurt.

"No, 'Pone. All I'm saying is, if we thought the Fortune Cookies were fakes, we wouldn't be helping the Ruhar."

"I guess," Jesse replied, disappointed by his friend.

"There's something else," Chisolm knew when to press an advantage. "The fact is, we aren't sure the Fortune Cookies are fakes. We don't know, and neither do you, not for certain. You switched your loyalty to the Ruhar because you think the Ruhar will treat UNEF better than the Kristang will, am I right about that?"

"So would you, if you opened your eyes," Jesse retorted.

"I agree with you." Chisolm said simply.

"Wait, what?" Jesse sputtered, disarmed.

"I agree the Ruhar will treat humans here better than the Kristang would have, if the Kristang had retaken this planet. The difference between you and me," Chisolm's eyes narrowed, "is *I'm* not thinking only of myself. We came out here to defend Earth; to protect the billions of people back home. Maybe the Kristang have betrayed us," his injuries prevented him from shrugging with his shoulders, so he used his eyebrows instead. "I accept the fact that I can't do anything to change the situation. What I *can* do is not give the Kristang any more reason to think of humans as untrustworthy. Everything we do out here reflects on humanity as a whole, and directly affects Earth. I have a family back home. To protect them as best I can, I am not going to give the Kristang a reason to hurt my family back home. I'm putting the billions of people on Earth before my own selfish interests."

Jesse wished he had tossed away the trash and gone directly back to the Buzzard.

"You want me to do something for you?" Chisolm addressed Dave. "Then answer a question; what do you think will happen when the Kristang on Earth find out a group of humans destroyed a Kristang battlegroup? Did the two of you ever think about the consequences to our people on Earth, or did you only think of what would be best for UNEF here?"

"The lizards on Earth won't find out about that." Dave stated confidently. "The wormhole to Earth is shut down. The lizards there have no idea what is happening out here."

Chisolm shook his head slowly, with pity for Dave. "You're sure about that?"

"The Ruhar told us. And the Kristang pretty much as admitted it," Dave retorted.

"And you are willing to bet the lives of your families back on Earth? That wormhole shut down suddenly. What happens if the wormhole reopens tomorrow?"

"Shit," Jesse said with disgust. "What if Santa Claus takes us all back to Earth in his sleigh tomorrow?"

"I'm not going to convince you today," Chisolm looked Jesse directly in the eyes. "I want you to think about it." With the corner of one eye, he saw Dave's head nod slightly. "What do you want from me?"

Dave was then unsure what he wanted, so he looked to Jesse.

What Jesse wanted to do right then was walk away, but seeing as talking with Captain Chisolm had been his idea, he plunged ahead. "There's a guy over there," Jesse jerked a thumb back over his shoulder. "Eric Koblenz, he's a Keeper. He was in our Company, then he lived in our village for a while." Until Eric pulled up stakes and moved to one of the unofficial Keeper villages. "If you ask me, Eric doesn't care about whether the Fortune Cookies are real or not, he doesn't think that deep. We had a sergeant in our village, a rabid-" Jesse realized using that word was not the best way to get Chisolm to help. "A 'dedicated' Keeper. This sergeant worked on Eric, and Eric became a Keeper because of that. Eric wasn't with us in Nigeria, he was a replacement brought in after we rotated back Stateside. He's always had a chip on his shoulder about not having been in Nigeria, and not ever having been in combat." Even on Paradise, when the Ruhar raided and then took back control of the planet, Eric had not seen any action. "Captain, Eric is a scared, stupid kid who thinks he has something to prove. He's throwing his life away."

Chisolm looked over Jesse's shoulder to the cluster of people standing under the shade of the hangar. Until that day, he had not met Eric Koblenz, and only knew of him from news on the zPhone network. "What do you want me to do?"

"He won't listen to us," Dave explained. "We were hoping you could talk to him?"

Chisolm's eyebrows raised in amused surprise. "You want me to persuade one of my fellow Keepers that I'm wrong, and he shouldn't come with us?"

Now that Chisolm said it, Jesse thought it was, indeed, a dumb request. "Look, Sir, if he's really sure of what he's doing, then he can go with my blessing. But if he's doing this because-"

"It doesn't matter," Chisolm stated. "All of us," he pointed to the assembled Keepers, "have fought against the Ruhar, or acted in a manner hostile to the Ruhar or UNEF. Eric never fired a shot, but he did participate in a raid that planned to capture weapons from a UNEF security patrol, then use those weapons against the Ruhar. The Ruhar intend to hold us in prison for the rest of our lives. Your friend may not be sure why he joined the Keepers of the Faith, but he is sure that going offworld with the Kristang is a better option than life in prison."

"Shit," Jesse breathed, deflated.

"He's not our friend," Dave said with a sad frown. "The guy's an asshole."

"He's a fellow soldier, and you're concerned about him," Chisolm clapped a hand on Dave's shoulder. "I admire that. Czajka, Colter; think about what I said. We came out here to protect Earth, not to make a better life for ourselves. I," he nodded as the Ruhar guards gestured for him to come with him. "I have to go."

"For what it's worth, Sir," Jesse snapped a very quick salute. "Via con Dios."

"You too, soldier. If we meet again, I hope it is under better circumstances."

Chisolm walked away, while Cornpone and Ski stood riveted in place. "Hell, *that* didn't go the way I planned," Jesse muttered. "I am a freakin' idiot."

"You think he's right?" Dave wondered uncertainly. "Not about being a Keeper. I mean, is he right that if we thought, or found out, that those Fortune Cookies were all a hamster trick, would we be on his side?"

"Shit," Jesse shook his head angrily. He liked things in life to be simple black and white. Captain Chisolm had complicated a subject that should have been starkly simple. "If the Ruhar have been lying to us all along, then we are well and truly, royally fucked, Ski. Because for damned sure, the lizards are no friends of ours."

CHAPTER FIVE

As they walked back to their Buzzard, a truck pulled up and Major Perkins got out. Jesse and Dave broke into a trot and reached the bottom of the ramp as Perkins did. "Trash run, Ma'am," Jesse explained, as he looked in dismay at the two new bags of trash an annoyed-looking Shauna had packed while they were uselessly arguing with Chisolm. "Did the Burgermeister say anything interesting?" They all by then called the Deputy Administrator 'Burgermeister'; Perkins had told them the Ruhar woman was fond of that nickname.

"Yes. She told me the commander of our arctic vacation reported we performed well, and I am to congratulate the team. I'll tell our pilots later. More importantly, we have another mission, and it's not the arctic again." Perkins did not mention the upcoming mission might be the very last time humans were allowed to do anything other than farming on Paradise. "We're going a quarter around the planet, to a projector site on a tropical island. It's going to be a long flight, so the Ruhar are giving us a special long-range Buzzard."

"A tropical island? Whoo-hoo!" Shauna exulted. "Should we pack swim suits, Ma'am?"

Frolicking in the ocean was something Perkins had not inquired about; there were dangerous predators in the oceans of Paradise, but swimming close to shore might be safe. She would like her team to be able to enjoy quality downtime, after they drilled a tunnel down to the projector and the Ruhar technicians were working to reactivate it. "That is a good question, Jarrett, I will ask our new Ruhar liaison."

"Liaison?" Jesse asked. "Who's that?"

Perkins explained. "We are all going to be on our very best behavior around our guest. The Deputy Administrator stuck her neck out for us, and she's asking a personal favor on behalf of her nephew. If this mission goes well, it may help his career as a cadet to have worked with us. If we screw something up, he'll catch part of the blowback and so will his aunt, and the stink will get all over us again."

Shauna looked distinctly unhappy. "This is not just a babysitting assignment, Major?" Shauna knew that if there was any babysitting to be done, the two female officers were of course not going to do it, and Jesse and Dave would assume babysitting was a woman's job. Which would mean Shauna inevitably getting stuck with the task.

"No," Perkins made a slashing motion with one hand. "Absolutely not. The Burgermeister made that clear to me. We could use a liaison officer, especially one who is well-connected," she added hopefully. "Um, she did say her nephew is a little awkward, I hope that means he's a normal Ruhar of his age. You'll receive a full briefing packet when-" She had noticed the pained and hurt expression on Dave's face. "Czajka, is something wrong?"

Dave looked at Jesse, who nodded. "Ma'am, when we were dumping trash, we, well-" Dave explained the mostly one-sided conversation they had with Captain Chisolm. While he was talking, he glanced at Shauna, embarrassed to appear so weak, so uncertain of himself. "I was just thinking, Ma'am, that Chisolm might be right. That if the Fortune Cookies are fakes, we've been all wrong about helping the Ruhar. Shooting up that battlegroup might have been the wrong thing to do."

"Captain Chisolm is right about that," Perkins replied, to the surprise of Dave and Jesse. Then she cocked her head. "People like Chisolm know they have to wrap their load of crap around a tiny kernel of truth, to hold it together. Yeah, I agree that *if* the Fortune

Cookies were planted by the Ruhar, then maybe we shouldn't have helped Emby destroy that battlegroup. I'll tell you this for certain: the Fortune Cookies are *not* fakes. They included multiple private authentication codes given to UNEF commanders before we left Earth. Because I was in Intel back then, I received a personal message for myself, in a Fortune Cookie. It was supposedly from my mother, and one thing she said was her dog had knocked a molasses bottle onto the kitchen floor, and the corners of her kitchen floor were still a sticky mess weeks later. That message wasn't from my mother; it was a code that I told UNEF Command to send, to authenticate messages. The rest of the message contained details of how the lizards were fucking over our home planet. That bit about molasses was known only to me, and UNEF Command on Earth, no one else. Unless the Ruhar were using magic, no way could they have known that. The idea of the Ruhar planting the Fortune Cookies assumes they somehow got past Kristang security, and Thuranin security, and altered the packaging on food that was loaded into Kristang containers on Earth. That makes zero sense," Perkins shook her head. "If the Ruhar wanted to screw with us, they could have planted DVDs or thumb drives or something, and faked messages that way."

"Makes sense," Dave mumbled quietly. "I'm sorry, Ma'am."

Emily Perkins nodded with sympathy. Sometimes she forgot how damned *young* her soldiers were. "Fanatics like Chisolm prey on people's uncertainties, and they know exactly how to manipulate people they want to recruit," she said, thinking Chisolm would have made a good intel officer. "And Chisolm is dead wrong, anyway. He said he's going with the Kristang, so they will have less of a reason to oppress our home planet? That is pure, one hundred percent bullshit. You know what we call giving in to a bully, so he won't hurt you as much? *Appeasement.* The United States military doesn't do appeasement, it never works. What Chisolm should be doing is what we're doing; building a relationship with a real ally. We don't need to play nice with the Kristang, we need to kick them in the teeth, and chase them the hell off our home planet. We need help from the Ruhar to do that. Us helping Emby destroy that battlegroup *was* the right thing to do; it told the lizards there are consequences to fucking with humanity."

Dave straightened up. Everything Major Perkins said made perfect sense, and more importantly, it *felt* right. Maybe that was why Emily Perkins was a major. "Yes, Ma'am. I'm clear about it now."

"Hooah," Jesse said, and bumped fists with Dave. "What's next, Ma'am?"

Perkins looked around. "We unload all our gear from our stolen Buzzard," the Ruhar security forces were still sore about that subject, but they had allowed Perkins and her team to keep flying the aircraft. And while they had been using it, the aircraft had acquired dents, scratches and minor broken bits and pieces from carrying a heavy drill rig that barely fit in the cargo compartment. She grinned. "We wouldn't get much for trading this thing in, I suppose. Good news is the Ruhar are allowing us to swap it for a new model. We'll be flying in a special long-range Buzzard for our next mission. Before we turn this one over to them, we clean it, scrub it top to bottom, so the Ruhar ground crew has less to complain about." Cleaning the Buzzard was a public relations gesture; Perkins was sure the Ruhar would overhaul the aircraft top to bottom. "This Ruhar liaison we're getting," she rolled her eyes, "will be arriving this afternoon. We'll need to have someone with this Buzzard at all times, until he shows up."

Dave was by himself in the Buzzard, when there was a knock on the Buzzard's composite skin near the open back ramp. "Hello?" It was a woman's voice.

Trouble on Paradise

Dave's head spun around, and he bumped into a structural frame. He had been cleaning nooks and crannies, getting the Buzzard ready to be returned to the Ruhar. "What? Ohhh," he added in a low voice. "Wow. Uh, hi?" His voice uplifted to end in a nervous squeak. It was woman. A real, live, human woman. Attractive, with short light blonde hair. And best of all, her French Army infantry uniform indicated she was an enlisted Caporal, not an officer. Before realizing what he was doing, he nervously ran a hand through his hair, smearing lubricating oil through his hair and on his forehead.

"Specialist Czajka?" The woman asked with a bemused smile in a charming accent.

Dave was instantly, head over heels in love. "Uh, yeah," He frantically looked around for a towel, not finding one close by. He stuck out a hand. "Dave Czajka."

She looked at his oil-covered hand.

"Oh," Dave caught her meaning. "Uh, give me a," he dug around in a toolbox until he located a clean rag, and scrubbed his hands as best he could. Probably best not to offer a handshake anyway. "Sorry about that. How can I help you, Caporal," he checked her nametag, "Bardot?"

"I was sent here to bring someone to the flight operations building, your new Ruhar liaison officer is there."

"Oh, yeah, I mean, yes, that is great. The others, Major Perkins, will be back here in-" Dave forgot what he said after that; it was a blur of babbling nonsense. He might have complimented Bardot on her hair, or something else about her appearance, although her baggy fatigues likely prevented much opportunity for him to embarrass himself in that direction. He might have bragged that he was on the team that destroyed a Kristang battlegroup, just in case she wasn't aware of that widely-known fact. He might have suggested they get together for lunch. It is possible that real, normal boy-girl date might have been proposed. About the only thing Dave was certain of is that he didn't get on his knees and beg her to please, please not leave.

"Dave, you are a nice guy," she interrupted him when he finally took a breath and let her speak, pronouncing the last word as 'ghee'. "It is, um, I like women?" She tried to let him down gently.

"Of *course* you're a lesbian," Dave said with disgust, rolling his eyes and pounding his fists together.

"What is *that* supposed to mean?" She asked, her friendly expression vanishing in an instant.

"I-"

"Because I am in the military? Or because I have short hair?" She demanded as she ran a hand through her bob cut. "Many women have-"

"No, no!" Dave waved his hands frantically. "All I meant is, of course you don't like men, because that is just the kind of rotten freakin' luck I have. Look, there's not many women on this entire planet. Instead of staying in Lemuria where I might meet someone, I've been flying around the planet in a Buzzard. We have three women on our team. Two are officers, and one of them we think is hooking up with another officer. Then there's Shauna, and she's with Jesse. Here we are, at a Ruhar airbase, and I finally meet a woman, and you don't like men. My life *totally* sucks."

"*Your* life sucks?" She said acidly. "How do you think I feel? I'm on a planet with very few women, and the women here all have their choice of men. If you think *you* have a tough time meeting women who might be interested in you, imagine how it is for me."

"Oh, shit," Dave's face fell, stricken. "Hey, I'm sorry." He awkwardly offered her a fist bump, and to his relief she responded. "I feel you. I mean-"

"I know what you meant that time," she said with a reassuring smile.

Craig Alanson

"Thanks." If he could have melted right through the floor and disappeared, he would have. "Listen, it's just that-"

"Hey, Dave," Shauna rescued him by popping her head in the side door. "Do you have, oh, hi. Who's your friend?"

"Caporal Giselle Bardot. You are Shauna?" She guessed. "I am here to bring your team to meet the new liaison officer."

"There he is," Bardot announced, pointing to a young Ruhar walking toward them. From the right, Major Perkins was also headed toward the alien. They met at about the same time. Although young, as a Ruhar he was still tall, already as tall as Dave. His face had not filled out yet, making his incisor teeth even more prominent, giving him an awkward, even goofy look to the humans. Shauna had to remind herself that this Ruhar was an advanced, genetically-enhanced being compared to humans. "Hello, Ms. Bardot," he waved enthusiastically at the French woman. "I am Nert Dandurf," he said to the group in general, with a smile that displayed his large front incisors even more prominently.

"Nert Dandruff?" Dave guessed.

"Dan-durf," Giselle corrected him.

"Oh, Dan*durf.* I am Dave Czajka." He stuck out a hand before remembering most Ruhar did not like touching lowly humans.

Nert shook his hand vigorously, squeezing hard enough to make Dave wince. "You are the one your fellows call 'Ski'?"

"Yes," Dave agreed, taken back by the Ruhar's knowledge.

"You must be Major Perkins," Nert snapped a proper Ruhar salute, which was touching two fingers of the left hand to his cheek.

Perkins returned the salute in US Army fashion. "I am pleased to meet you, Cadet Dandurf."

Nert made a slight bow. "I am honored to be part of your team, Major Perkins. Your exploits," he paused to see if that word translated correctly," are legendary already."

"We simply did our duty," Perkins said humbly.

"Your team destroyed a *battlegroup*," his face reflected both awe and hero worship. "While my people were, I think the expression is, sitting around with our thumbs up our asses?"

Perkins could not help laughing at his goofy grin. "We were presented an opportunity, and we made the most of it."

"You are too modest, Major Perkins," Nert's expression turned serious. "You are Specialist Jarrett?" He asked Shauna.

"Shauna Jarrett, yes. I am pleased to meet you, Cadet Dandurf."

"Please, call me Nert," he asked, unaware what his name sounded like to American ears.

Jesse hustled out of the flight operations building, arriving just as Nert finished speaking. "Hi," Jesse stuck out a hand, "I am Jesse Colter."

"Oh, Specialist Colter?" Nert's eyes lit up with delight. "Yes, you are the male person who is knocking boots with Specialist Jarrett," Nert smiled, pleased to know so much about the team of humans he would be working with.

Shauna gasped and shot a hurt look at Jesse. "Hey," Jesse protested quickly, "*I* didn't say anything! Listen, Shauna and I are not-" He froze. Everyone on the team knew he and Shauna had a relationship. He couldn't deny they were involved. "We're not doing anything with our boots," he thought that was a safely neutral thing to say.

"Oh," Nert was puzzled. "I understood the human term 'knocking boots' to be a reference to mating rituals. That did confuse me; I do not see why boots would be involved. I thought human genitals were located," he pointed to his crotch, "rather than on your feet."

"Yes!" Jesse cut him off, mortified at the turn the conversation had taken.

"Ah," Nert nodded. "Boots, then, are an aid in pleasurable copulation?" He asked, his face displaying complete innocence.

"No," Jesse's face was beet red, and Shauna was hiding her face behind her hands in horrified shock. "We don't, uh," he glanced from Perkins' bemused expression to Dave, who was trying not to choke from laughing. "We don't use boots, it's an express-"

"Perhaps the human male mates with the boot, rather than with the female?" Nert pointed to Jesse. "Although, your boots are large, I did not think you were so well endow-"

"Cadet Dandurf!" Major Perkins had to halt the discussion, before she burst into laughter at the social awkwardness of their new alien liaison officer. "Your knowledge of human language and social customs is impressive." She was not lying, except that Nert's knowledge of social customs had some major gaps. "Who taught you about these, uh, social customs?"

Nert's face beamed. "Two very nice men from your American Third Infantry helped me. I learned much from them."

"Uh huh," Perkins sighed. "Colter, Czajka, give Cadet Dandurf a tour of our Buzzard, and find out what else those jokers from the Third mistaught him. Jarrett, you're with me, I think the conversation they need is guys only."

The Kristang special forces unit designated '39 Commando', who previously had disguised themselves as the '134th Operational Support Company', struggled to pull the camouflage netting off their Jawkuar stealth dropship during a driving rainstorm at night. At the end of the desperate ground battles to control the planet's projector network, the cold-hearted commandos had lured the Ruhar in to wipe out an unwitting group of Kristang soldiers who had been used as decoys, so that the real 39 Commando could slip away undetected. Since that battle, they had huddled in the dense jungle of the southern continent, living in and around their Jawkuar, waiting for an opportunity that would be worth sacrificing the elite commando unit. A few hours earlier, the commando leader had found the opportunity they had been looking for. "We have a chance to hit the Ruhar very badly, and the timing is fortuitous," the commando leader told his squad leaders, as they waited for the Jawkuar to complete powering up for flight. "It will be a long, slow flight." The Jawkuar dropship had been designed for maximum stealth, intended for inserting special operation teams behind enemy lines. Exactly the sort of missions 39 Commando had been trained for. The Jawkuar could wrap itself in a sophisticated stealth field, its heat signature could be temporarily masked by dumping waste heat into an internal heat sink, and it was sleekly aerodynamic; its flight still disturbed the atmosphere it flew through. The Jawkuar had special fans at the rear of its wings and tail, fans which smoothed out the airflow to return the surrounding air to its original state, whatever that was. All those features, which significantly compromised the Jawkuar's combat capability, could still not allow the dropship to remain undetected if it flew too fast. So, for stealth operations, the Jawkuar flew low and slowly. "Most of the flight will be over deep ocean, where the Ruhar do not have a ground sensor network; we can increase speed there." The leader pointed to a map on the display. "This is our objective."

One of the squad leaders, bolder than the others, sniffed in a Kristang expression of surprise. "*That* is our target? There is nothing there worth our time."

"No," the leader's lips curled. He appreciated a certain amount of boldness in his squad leaders. "This is our *objective*. Our *target* is elsewhere."

The squad leader perhaps regretted his earlier boldness, aware the commando leader was playing with him. "Esteemed Leader, I do not understand."

"Our objective," the leader adjusted the display for a closer view, "is where we will find the means to strike the enemy. We will strike a blow the enemy will remember for a very long time. And we will wipe the smug smiles off their well-satisfied, furry little faces."

Ski lifted clothes out of his dufflebag; he needed to remove his cold weather gear and pack for a tropical climate. Looking at the battered canvas, he considered how far the dufflebag had traveled with him. To Nigeria and back. To Camp Alpha, and now Paradise. This was the third planet the bag had been on. While Dave himself had lost weight on a restricted diet, and he had picked some scars since he left Earth, he was better off than the dufflebag. If he had to stitch up another rip in a seam, he may as well use the dufflebag's canvas for scrap and try to get a replacement.

As he removed items from the dufflebag and stacked them carefully on a jump seat, a small vacuum-packed clear plastic pouch fell to the deck. Before Ski could grab it, Jesse picked it up and examined it. "What is this?"

Dave snatched it from his friend's hand. "It's my lucky underwear."

Jesse, of course, did not question there being such a thing as lucky underwear. "How are they lucky?"

"They're not, not yet."

"Huh?"

Ski held up the sealed plastic pouch. "This is my one clean pair of underwear, on this whole planet. If I ever think there is *any* chance that I might get lucky, I'm making sure to be wearing these."

"Oh. I got you," Jesse said, holding his fist out for a bump.

Dave returned the gesture. "The shorts I'm wearing right now have so many holes, the only reason they haven't dissolved is the cotton molecules are holding hands."

"So, they're just starting to get broken in?" Jesse grinned.

"To you and me, yeah. Girls don't understand that. If you get that far, and a girl sees you've got a ratty pair of shorts, she may change her mind. No way am I taking that chance."

"I hear you," Jesse held out a fist and Dave bumped it. "When you're done packing, we need to educate our new friend Nert. He's up in the cockpit, playing with the flight simulator."

"Good! That's good, Nert, you got it. That was perfect," Jesse praised their new liaison officer.

"Thank you, Specialist Colter," Nert said, beaming a buck-toothed smile with pride.

"Nert, call me Jesse," he offered. That was less awkward than 'Specialist Colter' and would hopefully prevent Dave from suggesting the Ruhar refer to him as 'Cornpone'. Jesse didn't mind his team using that nickname, but he didn't like it for general usage.

"Call me Dave," Ski agreed. "Hey, Nert, now we'll show you how to offer a gesture of praise, for people who have done a particularly good job."

Trouble on Paradise

Nert tilted his head, listening intently to the translation through his earpiece. "People who have performed a task with notable effort or skill?"

"Uh, yeah," Dave looked at Jesse. Nert sounded like a nerd partly because the translator made everyone's language awkward. "Now, look, you hold your left arm in front of you like this, no, don't hug it to your chest. Hold it away from you a bit. Then you bring your right arm up, with your hand outside your left forearm, right! Pump your right fist up and down, that's it," Dave struggled to keep a straight face as Nert happily performed an 'up yours' gesture. "Uh huh. Up and down like that, when you do it like that, you are showing your enthusiasm for the good job someone did."

Jesse broke into a coughing fit, to mask the laughter he could no longer contain.

"Thank you, Dave and Jesse," Nert said with the slight nod and bow the Ruhar used to express gratefulness. A group of three humans were crossing between hangars fifty meters away; Nert called out to them. "Hello!" He shouted without using the translator, and grinned as he used the friendly gesture he had just learned. "Good job!"

"What the hell?" One of the three guys stared at Nert. Jesse held up his hands, and Dave took a step away from Nert, twirling finger near his head to indicate Nert was crazy. "Hey!" The guy shouted back, returning the gesture. "Up yours too, buddy!"

"Thank you!" Nert kept pumping his fist up and down. "Good job!"

"Ok, Ok, that's enough for now, Nert. You don't want to overdo it," Jesse advised, gently pushing the alien's fist downward. Dave was almost doubled over, convulsed with laughter.

"I understand," Nert said happily. "What else can I-" Just then, Perkins came around the side of the Buzzard, with Shauna right behind her. Nert's face lit up. "Major Perkins! Good job-"

"NOOOO!" Dave and Jesse almost tackled Nert in their haste to stop him from giving his newly-learned gesture to their commanding officer.

Perkins stopped short. "What is going on here?"

"Uh, Ma'am, uh," Dave stammered, "we were, um," he shot a pleading look at Jesse who was of no help at all, "comparing interspecies methods of communication?" It sounded completely lame even to him.

"Uh huh," Perkins said slowly, not convinced.

"Did I do something wrong?" Nert asked unhappily.

"No, Nert, you didn't do anything wrong," Jesse assured their liaison officer. "You don't, uh, we don't use that salute with officers."

Shauna cocked her head, hands on her hips. "What have you two idiots been teaching him?"

Before Jesse or Dave could stop him, Nert did the 'up yours' gesture to Shauna. "Good job, Specialist Jarrett!" He said with grinning enthusiasm.

In spite of her better judgment, Major Perkins laughed and so did Shauna. Nert's goofy grin was so funny they couldn't help but laugh. "Nert," Shauna explained, "that gesture does not mean 'good job'. It is a, we would call it a rude gesture."

Nert was instantly crestfallen. "Dave and Jesse taught me wrong?"

"No, Nert," Shauna gave the two men a scathing look. "They were teasing you, that's all. Sometimes, humans tease a new member of a team, as a way of saying that new person is accepted as part of the group? You understand?"

Nert looked at his feet, miserable. "You do not like me?" He asked in a hurt voice.

Jesse's panic went to DEFCON 1 when he saw the look Shauna was giving him. She regarded their young alien cadet with almost motherly affection, and Jesse had made Nert feel bad about himself. "Oh, God, Nert, I am so sorry. We didn't mean anything by it, we were just joking around, you know? Please forgive-"

"Ha!" Nert looked up, bouncing on the balls of his feet. "I got you! I got you!" He exulted, winking at Shauna.

Jesse gasped, open-mouthed. "You son of a bitch. You son of a *bitch*! You did get me, that was a good one!"

"We friends now?" Nert asked without the translator.

"Oh, hell, yes," Jesse stuck out a hand to shake, and Dave did the same. "Welcome to the team, partner."

"You are going to fit in well with us," Dave assured the cadet.

CHAPTER SIX

"Hold it, all right, I, I got it. There." Jesse focused the Ruhar telescope that night, and pressed the button to transit the image to the zPhones of Dave and Shauna. It was their last opportunity for a while to view the Ruhar battlegroup in orbit; the last few ships would soon be departing for an exercise outside the star system.

"Wooo," Dave whistled. "This is a *big* MFer." Even with the image stabilization feature built into the telescope, the image was jumping around on the tablet screen. Ruhar, with their genetic enhancements, had finer control over their muscles; the telescope had not been built with the shaky hands of lowly humans in mind. "You think that is bigger than that Kristang battlecruiser we blew up, with that first projector shot? The, uh, what was the name of that ship?"

"*He Who Pushes Aside Fear Shall Always be Victorious*," Jesse answered.

"Oh, yeah." Dave snorted. "Always, huh? That name didn't work for those lizards."

"Screw them," Jesse had no sympathy for the Kristang, even if the crew of the *Victorious* had been vaporized in a sneak attack. "The database says that Ruhar ship up there is a battleship, the *Tos Blendaro*."

Dave laughed. "I wonder if her crew calls her the '*Blender*'?"

Jesse laughed too. "I don't think 'blender' means the same thing in Ruhar. Tos Blendaro is the name of a Ruhar planet, according to the database."

The three silently contemplated the giant alien battleship orbiting over their heads. "Hey, Cornpone."

"Hey, Ski. What's up?"

"I was just thinking. When I first heard Bish stole a dropship and went off on a crazy mission to hit the Kristang, I thought that was typical Bishop, you know? A stupid idea that had no chance of working. Like, what the hell could a group of humans in one dropship do against the Kristang, right? Then, we flew around this planet in one little Buzzard, and blew the hell out of an entire freakin' *battlegroup*. Now I'm thinking, what the hell? Maybe Joe actually did something useful up there. Maybe it wasn't just a signature Bishop grand gesture."

"Joe would do that?" Shauna asked. Although she had spent private time with Joe Bishop, she was realizing she didn't really know him like his former fireteam mates did.

"Oh yeah, Shauna," Dave assured her. "Joe is all about the grand gesture."

"Especially if it's stupid," Jesse agreed.

"Really?" Shauna considered that she hadn't ever known Joe at all, not really.

"Like using an ice cream truck against a Ruhar assault team?" Dave mentioned.

"Hey, for Bish, that was a *smart* idea," Jesse observed. "Jumping on top of an antitank mine to save us in Nigeria, now that was a classic Bishop futile grand gesture."

"Yeah. You know, though," Dave titled his head in thought. "If stealing that dropship and going after the Kristang really was a grand gesture, Joe wouldn't have brought volunteers along with him. He wouldn't have risked other people's lives. He must have thought the plan, whatever it was, had a real chance to succeed."

"Oh, come on, Ski," Jesse scoffed. "You still think Bish was in command of that op?"

"Yes, why? He was a colonel."

"Bish was a colonel like I'm a colonel," Jesse shook his head. "Promoting him was a publicity stunt, he knew that better than anybody. He was a figurehead. That's what he was on that op. No freakin' way could Joe ever figure out how to steal a Ruhar dropship.

And him plan an assault? Against Kristang ships? No way. Somebody else was in command; they used Joe as window dressing."

"You think that really was a UNEF special forces operation?" Shauna asked. "UNEF says they didn't know anything about it."

"Yeah, and that's what they would say, if it went south," Jesse turned the telescope off; the Ruhar battleship was sliding below the horizon. "Odds are the Ruhar were in command of that op; they needed humans as cover, or something like that. It's the only explanation that fits them using a dropship. No way in hell any humans could steal a dropship. Just to fly our stolen Buzzard, Lt. Striebich needed Emby to grant her access. I can guarantee there were Ruhar involved in Joe's op, somewhere along the line."

"That makes sense," Shauna agreed. She hadn't given the subject much thought.

"Anyway," Dave pulled up the collar of his jacket against the chill of the night, "I guess it's possible that Bish did something good up there."

"Yeah, before he got himself killed," Jesse added quietly.

"Why do you say that?" Shauna asked.

Jesse took one last look at the sky. A sky filled with hostile aliens. "He's not here, is he? Where else could he go? A dropship can't fly all the way back to Earth."

Two members of Major Perkins' team were entirely happy to hear about their new assignment. More than happy, they were thrilled. Pilots Irene Striebich and Derek Bonsu were thrilled to hear they would continue to fly. And not only fly, this time they got to fly a special, modified, long-range version of the Buzzard transport. The hull was stretched, which meant they could fit the drill rig, plenty of spare parts, and the team would not be squashed between the drill rig and the cockpit. This Buzzard even had seats that lay completely flat for sleeping, and a fully-equipped tiny galley. Compared to their arctic mission, this would be a luxury vacation.

Because the projector they were to reactivate was on an island far offshore, almost a quarter of the way around the planet, even the Buzzard's additional powercells would not provide enough range to get there and back. So, Irene and Derek had to not only be certified to fly the different type of Buzzard, they had to learn and become proficient at mid-air refueling. When the projector was fully operational and the Buzzards were on their return to base, a dropship would be descending from orbit to refuel them.

Irene did not have any doubts she could master flying the new type of aircraft; a Buzzard was a sweet bird to handle and a couple extra tons of mass weren't going to change its basic flight characteristics. Buzzard engines were overpowered, Irene knew the engines of her new ship would not have any problem carrying the drill rig, full crew and all their supplies. Nor was she worried about refueling in midair. She had done simulations of Ruhar procedures for aerial refueling, and the process was almost fully automated. The actual procedures she had witnessed were so simple a baby could do it. The 'baby' aircraft approached the 'mother' ship, and the mother ship took control of the baby's navigation; linking the two aircraft as one. The power connection then extended from the mother ship, guiding itself into the port on the aircraft to be refueled. Once connected, it took less than a minute to bring the baby's powercells up to full charge, then the connection retracted itself, and navigation control was restored.

The Ruhar in-flight refueling procedure was child's play compared to refueling operations Irene had done as a Blackhawk pilot. One time in a driving rainstorm over the Nigerian jungle at night, she had been nursing a stricken Blackhawk that was leaking fuel from shot-up tanks. The rate of fuel draining from the tanks was even greater than the rate of fuel being rapidly gulped by the one thirsty turboshaft engine that was still operational.

Trouble on Paradise

Irene had her one working engine screaming at full power as the helo lurched in a raging thunderstorm. Being over dense jungle under insurgent control, with no place to land and eight wounded soldiers, she would have run the tanks dry and crashed, except for a blessed angel appearing in the ungainly, fat form of a C-130 Hercules. It took her four tries, with the bullet-crazed cockpit windows lit up by the blinding strobe effect of lightning arcing through the clouds, to connect to the refueling drogue. The tanks were too leaky to top off, so she took on as much fuel as she could, then she was forced to disconnect from the refueling drogue as the wind shear grew too dangerous for the C-130. The Herc climbed to get above the dangerously roiling winds of the thunderstorm, but Irene had to fly through it; her own bird bouncing up and down hundreds of feet in the brutal winds. It was a race to see which would happen first; the thunderstorm blowing itself out, or the fuel tanks running dry and the turboshaft sputtering and dying. Or, Irene had thought to herself, another possible source of impending doom was the rotor blades over her head losing lift, as the Blackhawk was slammed toward the treetops by violent downdrafts.

She had survived that night, as did seven of the eight wounded soldiers she was carrying. The storm lessened enough for the C-130 to return, and she had been able to hook up for another half tank of fuel. When she landed on a dirt road miles from base, she had been soaked to the skin, and she had not been sure how much was from sweat, how much from rain splattering through bullet holes in the windows, or whether she had peed her pants in terror. If it were the latter, she wouldn't be ashamed. She had gone through forty minutes of thinking every moment would be her last, and her greatest fear had been getting her crew and the wounded soldiers killed.

That incident is what she thought of when she was taking simulator training for inflight refueling of a Buzzard. This shit is easy, she told herself without bravado. She would like to see a hotshot Ruhar pilot refuel a Blackhawk at night, even in good weather. Refueling a Blackhawk behind a C-130 Hercules, with the drogue being buffeted by the four spinning turboprops of the Herky Bird, and the Blackhawk's own whirling rotors. The Ruhar, she was certain, would pee their pants every time if they had to perform such a task in a primitive human aircraft.

The simulator gave her a passing rating, and Derek Bonsu also passed easily. The two humans didn't even have a silent, unspoken rivalry about their rating in the sim; the Ruhar refueling process was so laughably easy there was no point to a contest between them. The next step was an actual refueling test, aboard the actual Buzzard they would be flying on the mission. Irene and Derek gave their new ship a thorough inspection and found everything well-worn, and the maintenance logs indicated a long list of recent repairs. After their first checkout flight, Irene and Derek added a dozen 'squawks' in the log, noting problems they had found. The Ruhar crew chief was not happy to see more work added to his schedule. "You report the rear ramp would not fully extend in flight, until you cycled it twice. And then it would not seal properly after it was retracted? Why would *you*," he emphasized the last word scornfully, "ever need to open the ramp in flight?"

"We would need to open the ramp in flight," Irene explained with a patience she did not feel, "if the ship is in trouble, and we need to dump the drill rig to lighten our load. For example, over open water." She mentally added an unspoken 'you jackass'.

Their Ruhar flight instructor, who was not the most friendly person Irene had ever met, cut off the crew chief's scathing reply. "The human is correct. It must be fixed. The first eight items on the list must be fixed before we fly again. The other items are simple and should not take significant time to remedy."

"I will add this ship to the schedule," the crew chief glared at the flight instructor, feeling betrayed by his fellow Ruhar. "My crew is overworked," he swept a hand across the parked rows of aircraft and dropships needing maintenance before they could fly. Many of the aircraft still had battle damage that had only been cataloged, not even scheduled for repair. The battlegroup had brought in a wave of replacement aircraft, and most of them had a lengthy list of issues to be fixed before they could be considered flightworthy. As usual, Gehtanu got the unwanted leftovers from other Ruhar worlds. "We have combat aircraft that require priority attention. This ship," he rapped his knuckles on the composite fuselage, "will not be in the air again for ten days, if not longer."

"No," Nert declared quietly, and the crew chief raised an eyebrow. Until Nert spoke, the crew chief had not even acknowledged the young cadet's presence. "We have inflight refueling practice maneuvers scheduled for tomorrow. After tomorrow, the refueling dropship will not be available for another three days. The humans are needed for a mission of vital importance to the security of Gehtanu. This aircraft must be returned to flightworthy status by tomorrow morning."

"Cadet? Who are you to-" the crew chief began hotly.

"His aunt is Baturnah Logellia," the flight instructor explained. "And this little shit," he pointed to Nert, "will not hesitate to call her. I suggest you get your crews to work overnight, if necessary. I want a checkout flight one hour after sunrise, and there had better not be any additional problems, unless you want to find yourself fixing toilets."

Nert grinned, and winked at Irene and Derek. Irene gave him a half smile back. She didn't like pulling rank, especially when it involved politics. And particularly she did not like people using family connections to get favors. In this case, with the Ruhar openly biased against humans, she could not fault Nert for doing his job as their team's liaison. The Deputy Administrator wanted Major Perkins' team to begin their mission in three days; that meant Irene and Derek had to perform their inflight refueling test the next day. Any slip in the schedule would be an excuse for the Ruhar to remove humans from the projector mission.

The Buzzard was fully ready for flight the next morning. Irene knew that because the crew chief had 'helpfully' sent updates to her zPhone every half hour, while she was trying to sleep. After the third update, when she had been unable to silence her zPhone, she had tucked it under the mattress, and drifted off to a restful sleep. The crew chief had not been as resentful as she expected, partly she thought the Ruhar was proud that his crews had addressed all the squawks so quickly. The check ride, with the flight instructor at the controls and Irene in the copilot seat, went acceptably so they contacted the refueling dropship.

During the first actual refueling maneuver, behind a real dropship, Irene had been singing quietly to herself, even yawning with boredom. The Ruhar flight trainer made her and Derek each go through basic refueling process three times. Then he screwed with them. The instructor deactivated the flight computer, forcing Irene to fly manually. That was no problem for her; flying the big Buzzard on manual was easier than flying a Blackhawk. The instructor threw more problems at her; power failures, intermittent system glitches, complete loss of sensors at night. For that last scenario, Irene had calmly donned vision-enhancing goggles and flew smoothly to connect to the refueling cable on her first attempt. Finally, the instructor told Irene that the Buzzard had lost power to one engine, the second engine was on fire and the powercells had less than one percent remaining.

Trouble on Paradise

Irene pulled the Buzzard into a gentle turn away from the lumbering dropship, reduced the blazing engine to idle and activated the fire suppression system.

"What are you doing?" The flight instructor pointed anxiously at the dropship. "Your fuel state is critical! You must connect immediately or we will lose power permanently."

"Yes," Irene responded without looking at him. "With fire in one engine, procedure prohibits approaching the tanker ship, due to risk of explosion. If I am able to put out the fire, and the engine throttles up successfully, I can try to connect." She looked directly at him, since the instructor decided how the scenario would play out.

"Correct," the instructor avoided her eyes. "Striebich, I judge you have performed adequately. Derek Bonsu, take the pilot seat, it is your turn."

As Irene strapped into the jump seat next to Nert, she allowed herself a ghost of a smile. 'Performed adequately', she asked herself. Sure, she thought, like the sun *might* rise the next morning. She had aced the test, and she knew Derek would do the same.

Whether the internal politics of the Ruhar on Paradise would cancel the mission was something she had no control over.

The flight instructor refused to state whether he would mark Irene and Derek as ready to make a long overwater flight, in a new model of Buzzard. Major Perkins met her two pilots in the ready room her team had been assigned at the airbase. "Well? Lieutenant, did the instructor approve the two of you for flight?"

"I don't know, Ma'am," Irene admitted. "We did everything by the book. I think the instructor was pissed that we didn't break something. That asshole better not give me a taco on that exercise; we were freakin' perfect."

"Taco?" Nert asked, confused by the translation.

"An unsatisfactory rating begins with the letter 'U'," Derek explained while sketching a 'U' shape in the air with a finger. "A taco shell looks kind of like a 'U'."

"You passed, you will be approved," Nert interjected.

"You spoke with the instructor?" Perkins asked.

"Yes, but I didn't need to. The pilots did everything correctly, he can't justify failing them based on performance. Although I do think he wanted to. Major Perkins, my aunt wishes your team to fly this mission. Unless the pilots made a terrible error, they were guaranteed to pass."

"Great, thank you," Derek said sarcastically. "That makes me feel wonderful about it."

"Oh, no!" Nert rushed to add. "You both achieved more than a 95% score overall. I do not know the exact rating for either of you, all I can tell is you were rated," the translator stumbled over the word. Nert frowned, and looked up something on his zPhone. Then he spoke without the translator. "Your word is 'outstanding', I think is the correct translation?" He switched the translator back on. "The flight instructor told me he believes your success is due to the fact that you have been trained to fly your own primitive human aircraft, which is more difficult than flying a Ruhar aircraft. That makes up for your slow reflexes and general lack of coordination and fine muscle skills."

"Thank you, Nert," Irene said while rolling her eyes at Derek. "We appreciate the compliment."

"It is my pleasure, Lieutenant Striebich," Nert cluelessly beamed with pride.

Perkins rolled her eyes at that remark. "We have an aircraft, then. Jarrett reported the drill rig had been serviced and is ready and waiting for us. We need to get it checked out top to bottom, then loaded aboard the Buzzard, today."

"Ma'am," Irene looked stricken, "Bonsu and I got up at 0330, and it's been a stressful day. We were hoping to catch some rest."

"I understand that," Major Perkins said with sympathy. "Lieutenant, we need to make damned sure some Ruhar doesn't think it is his patriotic duty to remove us from this mission by sabotaging the drill rig, or our ability to carry it safely in the Buzzard."

Irene opened her mouth and quickly closed it. She had considered the possibility of sabotage or sloppy workmanship affecting her Buzzard, but she had given no thought to the drill rig itself. "Yes, ma'am."

"Jarrett is in Hangar Four with Czajka and Colter, go take charge over there," Perkins ordered.

"You're not coming with us, Major?" Derek asked, surprised. Perkins was typically a hands-on leader.

"I'll join you when I can. Right now, our liaison and I are going over to the Admin building, to assure there isn't some unfortunate paperwork glitch in you and Striebich getting signed off for flight duty."

Nert, listening to the translation in his zPhone earpiece, was puzzled. "Unlike humans, we do not use paper, Major Perkins. Our records are stored in-"

"I understand that, Cadet Dandurf. My meaning is that I intend to assure there are no unintended, or *intentional*, delays in getting their flight status officially logged into, whatever system stores that data."

"Ah," Nert nodded. "I understand. That would be wise." He knew many of his fellow Ruhar were not happy that humans were being given another opportunity. Especially as the humans were taking the place of Ruhar who would love to be on projector reactivation team. "And I believe that I know the person we must speak with."

"Great, Cadet. Lead the way."

Irene and Derek assumed Shauna Jarrett, who somehow along the way had become their drill rig expert, would merely check the rig's records, maybe look at the inspection tags, and roll it across the airfield to the waiting Buzzard. But no! Major Perkins had ordered Shauna to assure the drill rig was in perfect working order, and that is exactly what Shauna intended to do.

"Seriously?" Irene asked, eyes wide. "You want to drill into the airbase?"

"Irene, Lt. Striebich," she remembered that her friend Irene was also an officer. "We won't know for certain this thing works, unless we see it in action. Nert got us permission to drill into that stretch of grass over behind Hangar Five, there aren't any buried pipes or cables in that area."

"Oh," Derek groaned, "this is going to take all day!"

"No, sir," Jesse grinned. "We should be done in time for dinner."

"Yeah," Dave agreed. "Then we just need to get it over to the Buzzard, stowed away and secured. Oh, and all the spare parts have to get loaded and tied down. Shouldn't take longer than, what do you think, Cornpone? Midnight?"

Jesse whistled. "That may be ambitious, but we can try. Welcome to the Army, sir," He winked at Lt. Bonsu.

The pitifully few ships of Admiral Kekrando's once mighty, conquering battlegroup hung motionless in deep space, far from the star which bathed the planet Pradassis with warm, life-giving light. That far out, the ships could only be seen by their blinking navigation lights. The star was a mere dot, and Pradassis could not be seen by the naked eye. No, he could not call the planet 'Pradassis', Kekrando told himself. With the Ruhar having stationed a battlegroup there, and in the process of constructing a strategic defense satellite network around the planet, it would never again be called 'Pradassis' by anyone who lived there. Gehtanu. The planet would now forever be known as Gehtanu.

"All ships in formation, Admiral," said a voice behind Admiral Kekrando. The voice was quiet and hesitant, as it should be under such shameful circumstances. Shame did not belong directly to the speaker, being only the second in command of the destroyer, but the stench of Kekrando's overwhelming failure infected everyone around that unfortunate senior warrior.

"Very well," Kekrando acknowledged in a clear, strong voice. A voice accustomed to command. A voice unaccustomed to failure or shame. Until now. "Initiate compliance with Jeraptha docking requirements. All reactors in cold shutdown, except for the Auxiliary Power Units aboard each ship. Stealth and sensors fields deactivated, defensive energy shields on standby." The Jeraptha would not allow the powerful defense shields of the Kristang ships to be active for the docking procedure, but they understood ships would need to protect themselves from being impacted by random space junk, even at the far outskirts of the star system. "All weapons safed," he ordered, knowing even the defensive maser turrets were included in that category. Anything that might pose a threat to a massive Jeraptha star carrier had to be completely deactivated. The Jeraptha insisted maser cannons needed to have their exciters decoupled from their power supplies. All missiles must have detonators removed from warheads. "And, Kartow," Kekrando turned to stare at the destroyer's executive officer, "no cheating. Clan leadership had ordered me to deliver these ships back home in one piece. If the Jeraptha discover we are cheating, and if even one ship is cheating they *will* discover it, then consequences will be dire for all of us. Signal all ships," all ships that remain, he thought bitterly. "I do not want anyone trying to be a hero, or to claim glory for themselves. Is that understood?"

Kartow saluted. "Understood, Admiral," he said, then almost scurried away to pass along the admiral's commands. In truth, Kartow, like everyone else in the depleted battlegroup, wished to be as far away as possible from their disgraced admiral. Proximity carried the potential of Kekrando's shame spreading to others. For certainly, with a failure of such epic proportions, there was more than enough disgrace and shame for more than one person.

Kekrando stood with uncharacteristic silence as the crew busied themselves around him, no one daring even glance at the admiral, for fear his shame and eventual fate were contagious. Kekrando listened as his orders were passed along to the other ships. No cheating, he heard. Left to himself, he would have liked to cheat, to do more than just cheat. He would have liked to wait for the Jeraptha star carriers to emerge from jump and approach, then Kekrando would have opened up on them with every weapon his ships had. The result would have been the certain destruction of all his remaining ships, but possibly he could have severely damaged, even destroyed, one or both star carriers. Striking such a blow against the patrons of the Ruhar would have been an immensely satisfying, if futile and even counterproductive gesture. But it was not to be. Clan leadership had ordered Kekrando to bring his remaining ships safely home, where they would be needed for a Kristang civil war that was now all but inevitable. Loss of the combat power of one battlegroup was bad enough, worse still was the enormous loss of prestige for the clan. Such shame made it difficult for the clan to keep existing allies and attract new clans to an alliance, even a temporary arrangement. Kekrando's failure had made the entire clan appear weak. He could not blame other clans for their scorn; his had been a monumental failure, a disaster that would be studied for generations as an example of what *not* to do when in command of an isolated battlegroup. Kekrando knew the clan leaders had ordered his subordinate officers to relieve the admiral of command if he attempted to strike the Jeraptha, such relief would come in the form of a pistol round to the admiral's skull.

Kekrando had appeared in the skies over Pradassis with overwhelming combat power, instantly establishing supremacy in space around the planet. Nothing then could move within twelve lightminutes of Pradassis without Kekrando knowing and approving; and everything and everyone on the surface existed because he had wished them to continue existing.

He could have been forgiven for the loss of the majority of his ships; no one could have foreseen the Ruhar's use of unknown maser cannons. Even clan leadership, who of course would not be accepting any blame for themselves, would be reluctant to punish Kekrando for falling victim to a shocking, vicious, dishonorable sneak attack. What the clan leadership could not abide was what happened next. Even following the projector attack on Kekrando's battlegroup, he had sufficient combat strength to prevent Commodore Ferlant's Ruhar task force from effectively protecting the planet. And then Senior Captain Gerkaw's pursuit squadron, which needed merely to keep Ferlant's ships busy and away from the planet, had been foolishly lured into a trap by the wily Ruhar commander. The fact that the idiot Gerkaw had exceeded his orders made no difference to clan leadership. The failure ultimately belonged to the commanding officer on the scene: Admiral Kekrando.

Even Kekrando had to admit a greater disaster, a greater failure, could hardly be imagined. Clan leadership had sent him to Pradassis, to secure the planet and its buried Elder treasures for the clan. The riches of Elder artifacts could vault the clan to the upper ranks of Kristang society. Instead, the planet was now firmly in the control of the hated Ruhar, who had discovered a priceless, fully functional Elder power tap, and a pair of working comm nodes! The fact that the incompetent Ruhar had screwed with, and destroyed, the Elder devices made no difference to clan leadership. Those items beyond value should have been the property of the clan, and Kekrando's own stunning, monumental incompetence had given them away to the Ruhar.

Kekrando knew he likely faced death when he returned. Lesser commanders might have taken the easy way out, by using a pistol, a knife or even poison. Such cowardice was not for a proud warrior; Kekrando would face the clan leaders with his head held high, and offer whatever analysis and advice as he could, before meeting his fate. By retaining his dignity as a warrior, Kekrando hoped to save his ship captains from sharing his own fate.

"All ships acknowledge your orders, Admiral," Kartow announced from his duty station, not wishing to come any closer to the symbol of disgrace. "The Ruhar transport ships are in position; their defensive systems are active."

Kekrando answered only with a curt nod of his head. The presence of two Ruhar transport ships deeply puzzled him. Aboard those two ships were over six thousand, seven hundred humans who referred to themselves as 'Keepers of the Faith'. The admiral could understand why the Ruhar had agreed to transport the troublesome Keepers away from their planet; sending those pesky humans away would reduce the security burden on the Ruhar. He could not yet understand why clan leadership had agreed to accept the humans; Kekrando could not see how such primitive, untrustworthy creatures could possibly be useful to the clan. Human soldiers, even the best of them, hardly offered enough of a challenge to make hunting them enjoyable sport. Perhaps the clan leadership intended the humans to be used for training young Kristang warriors to hunt with knives and bare hands. Or perhaps clan leadership planned to sell humans to other clans as curiosities, or for sport. No matter, that was not Kekrando's concern.

No, what puzzled him most was why the 'Keepers' had volunteered to leave Pradassis with the Kristang. If they thought their continued display of loyalty impressed their patrons, they were greatly, fatally mistaken. Seeing humans divided between loyalty to the Ruhar and Kristang only reinforced the Kristang's firmly-held opinion that humans were weak. Kekrando could only imagine that the 'Keepers' were the type of rigid-thinking creatures who could not accept reality when their beliefs were challenged; could not adapt as all living things must. Adapt, if they wished to continue living.

One thing Admiral Kekrando was certain of was, that the almost seven thousand Keepers would not continue living very long.

CHAPTER SEVEN

39 Commando's Jawkuar altered course to fly into a rain squall. Such brief, intense rain storms were common over the tropical ocean, but the Jawkuar crew had found squalls frustratingly sparse that day. The heat sinks in the belly of the dropship had been approaching critical temperature, and need to be ejected soon, or the all-important stealth would be compromised. As the dropship flew into the storm, the pilots allowed it to be buffeted by the gusty winds, for using power to stabilize the Jawkuar's flight path might be detected.

Once the dropship was fully within the squall cloud, its skin pelted by fat raindrops, the copilot activated controls to eject the heat sinks. A door briefly opened on the belly of the dropship, and two objects dropped out. After falling a few meters, parachutes opened to slow their descent, because a speedy fall of such heavy objects might be detected. Each heatsink was surrounded by a thermal insulation shell, trapping the heat inside. Within the shell, the heatsinks were far beyond their melting point, and the shells would not survive long. They did not have to. Within a few minutes, the heatsinks hit the ocean surface with a gentle splash, the parachutes retracted, and the heatsinks began falling toward the bottom of the sea. The two shells failed around the same time, within seconds of each other. Cracks appeared, and when the contents of the shells leaked out, the ocean water flashed into steam. By then, the heatsinks were safely deep enough that the event was not noticed by the Ruhar sensor network.

Above the waves, the Jawkuar flew smoothly out of the rain squall into clear air. If any Ruhar had been close by, they would have wondered why water was falling from a clear patch of sky, as water dripped off the Jawkuar's surface. Satisfied the heatsink ejection had not detected, the pilots turned back to their original course and increased speed slightly. Excess heat was now being dumped into two new heatsinks, and the pilots watched the instruments carefully. The Jawkuar had only a limited number of heatsinks, which could not be reused. Luck would have to be with them on this mission.

Ruhar personnel at the airbase watched with curiosity, or disdain, or a mixture of both as the odd human creatures drove the drill rig behind a hangar. The humans not only practiced setting up and taking down the drill, they actually fitted a bit to the drill and began chewing down into the soil. Every Ruhar on the base knew this group of humans had a mission to reactivate one of the last projectors. The humans might be crude, they might be paranoid, but no one could say they were not taking their mission very seriously. The humans were absolutely thorough about making certain the rig was ready for the mission, even the Ruhar who hated humans as occupier lackeys of the Kristang had to admit this particular team of humans was admirably professional. The drill was operating normally for the first twenty feet, then Shauna began tapping the display on her zPhone with concern.

"Cut! Jesse! Cut the power! Now!" Shauna shouted frantically, waving her arms.

Jesse complied. "Ok! Done. What's the problem?" All the instruments on the console in front of him were showing green. Not green, exactly, because the Ruhar used the color blue instead of green to indicate things were working properly. Both humans and Ruhar used red to indicate a problem, and there was no red on the console in front of Jesse. "Everything shows normal here."

"Normal now, it wouldn't be normal if we'd kept going," Shauna insisted. "Look at the temperature of the upper coupling."

Jesse checked it, looked at Dave for confirmation, and Dave nodded. "It's running a little hot," Jesse admitted. "Still within normal limits."

"Run the instrument data back," Shauna walked over to the console and ran the instrument data backward, then let it display forward. "See?" She stabbed a fingertip on the display. "It starts perfectly normal, then here, right here, it spikes. And keeps going."

Dave's eyes grew wide. "Sorry, Shauna, I was only looking for trouble. My attention was on the drill head."

Jesse hung his head. Shauna was right, the coupling temperature had spiked, and he hadn't noticed it on the console. Shauna had been monitoring the drill rig's sensors through her zPhone, and she had seen it. Even now, with the rig's power cut off, the coupling temperature was still increasing. "Hey, this is screwy," he noticed. "The temperature gauge of the coupling shows it's fine, we're getting a high temperature reading from the housing itself. I don't get it."

"Me neither," Shauna replied, her jaw set. "This drill rig is supposed to have been completely refurbished for us. The chief mechanic signed off that it was ready."

Irene exhaled in exasperation. "Jarrett, it's a good thing you insisted on an operational test." She hated to admit it, but making the drill rig crawl behind the hangar, and setting it up to drill into the ground had been well worth the time and effort. They had drilled barely thirty feet down before Shauna had detected the problem.

"Lt. Striebich, I'd like to look inside," Shauna said hopefully.

"I don't know, Jarrett," Irene said uncertainly. A group of Ruhar had been watching the drill rig from the back door of a hangar; now one of them was headed in their direction. "We're not supposed to screw with Ruhar equipment."

"It was the freakin' Ruhar who told us this thing was in perfect condition," Shauna pointed out. "We can't trust them."

"She's right about that," Derek agreed.

"Oh, hell," Irene muttered. "How much more trouble could we get into? Jarrett, pop this thing open."

Shauna moved quickly. She had Jesse and Dave lower the rig horizontally so she could access the upper coupling. Even before it had completed lowering itself, she hopped onto a grating and turned two levers to open an inspection hatch. Seeing that, the Ruhar coming from the hangar broke into a run. "Damn it!" Shauna shouted, her left arm inside the rig up to her shoulder. She pushed hoses out of the way, until she had a good view of the lubricant reservoir.

Just as the Ruhar stomped across the grass, angrily waving his arms and shouting at Shauna, a car roared up to the drill rig, and Major Perkins and Nert got out. "What is the problem here?"

"I am a mechanic," the angry Ruhar explained through a zPhone translator. "Your people have interfered with-"

"We had to shut down the rig around thirty feet, Major," Irene reported. "Jarrett noticed a problem, a coupling was overheating."

"This is bullshit. Total *bullshit*!" Shauna spat angrily.

"What is the problem?" Major Perkins repeated, peering over Shauna's shoulder.

"This," Shauna tapped a clear bottle that was barely visible behind a complicated array of pipes and hoses. "I noticed the upper coupling gearbox was running hot, but the instruments said there was plenty of this lubricating fluid being sprayed onto this coupling here, see this?"

Perkins couldn't actually see much, with Shauna's arm in the way. "And?"

"And, ma'am, this fluid reservoir is empty, even though the instruments say it's full. That's what clued me in to look; the fluid level should have dropped a little while the drill was operating."

"Can you remove the reservoir?" Perkins asked.

"I can do it, but this gentleman here," she pointed at the enraged Ruhar, "says we humans are not authorized to perform maintenance on this machinery. I wasn't even supposed to open this inspection hatch, even though," she glared back at the Ruhar, "it is a *hatch* that is designed to *open* so you can *inspect* the inside of the rig."

Perkins nudged Shauna aside gently, so she could get a better view inside the hatch. "Remove it."

It was an awkward move, but the reservoir was designed to be easily replaced, so Shauna's nimble fingers were able to get the retaining clips undone, then she rotated it ninety degrees until it came loose. "Son of a *bitch*," she spat as she pulled it out of the hatch. "Look, the fluid level indicator here is jammed, stuck. That's why it read full, when it was empty. I, oh, shit." She handed the clear bottle to Perkins. "Someone messed with it, Major. The indicator has glue or something holding it to the full position."

Perkins examined the reservoir closely, then held it out for the others to see. "Yes, I see it. It looks like glue, it could be some residue, if the fluid dried out and congealed."

"No way, ma'am," Dave said, shaking his head. "That little dot of glue is dark blue. The lubricant fluid is pink. Shauna's right, ma'am, this is total bullshit."

Perkins shook the reservoir suspiciously. A few drops of light pink fluid ran down the inside of the bottle. "This is odd. Sabotaging the reservoir would not have prevented us from participating in this mission," she observed. "We wouldn't have known about it until, oh, shit."

"Yes," Shauna stated. "It's worse. We would have flown all the way out there and busted the drill. This coupling is one component we don't carry a spare for; it's integrated with the housing and the motor. If the coupling burned out, it would be faster and easier for the Ruhar to fly out a new drill."

"A new drill, with a Ruhar crew to operate it," Perkins glared at the Ruhar mechanic. "Because the stupid humans burned out their own drill. I get it. As sabotage goes, this was reasonably smart." She turned to Nert. "Cadet, can you inquire whether there are spare reservoirs like this on the base?"

"Oh," Nert fairly bounced on his toes with eagerness to show his knowledge. "Yes. Yes, there are spares. This is a common component used in our trucks and aircraft."

"Excellent. Please arrange to have three reservoirs delivered, and my team will install one of them."

"No!" The mechanic protested. "I will replace-"

Perkins' wrath focused on the mechanic. Although he was more than a head taller than her, she stepped forward until they were toe to toe and she was glaring up into his brown eyes. "I am Major Emily Perkins. What is your name?"

"Slonn Janes. I am a master mechanic," he replied stiffly.

"Mr. Janes, this is my team, I am responsible for the success of this mission. *My* team will replace the reservoir. I take full responsibility for any damage to the drill rig."

"It is not necessary-"

"This could be sloppy workmanship, or it could be incompetent workers, or it could be sabotage," she paused for the translation to catch up. "Either way, this is a very serious matter. This incident can either be reported up to the highest level," she looked meaningfully at Nert, knowing the mechanic likely knew who the cadet was related to.

"Or, we can assume this is a simple mechanical failure, and take care of it ourselves, right here. Right now."

In one way, Ruhar culture was like human culture. Neither species liked higher authorities to be notified about problems, if it could be avoided. The mechanic spoke slowly so the translator could keep up, and he could see Perkin's reaction to his words. "There is no need to involve anyone other than myself."

"I would appreciate it if a master mechanic, such as yourself, would show my team how to properly install the replacement reservoir." She stepped back from Janes, smiled, and softened her tone. "If there is a problem with another reservoir during our mission, we will need to replace it in the field, by ourselves."

That made sense to Janes. "Major Emily-"

"Major *Perkins*," Nert interjected unhelpfully.

"Major Perkins," Janes tried again, "I will instruct your team in the proper procedure for replacing the fluid reservoir. And," he glanced at Nert, "I will investigate how a malfunctioning component was installed by *my* team." Janes appeared genuinely embarrassed and angry. Impulsively, he stuck out a hand, and Perkins shook it briefly. Briefly, because she was sure the Ruhar did not enjoy touching a human.

Master Mechanic Slonn Janes kept his word. He showed Shauna how to replace the reservoir, and supervised as she instructed Jesse and Dave how to do it. Then, with the mechanic assisting, and a half dozen idle and curious Ruhar watching, they set the drill rig upright again and put it back in action, drilling down to one hundred feet in the relatively soft soil.

"Jarrett," Perkins asked their de facto drill rig expert three hours later, "are you satisfied with the performance of this rig?"

"Yes, ma'am," Shauna replied wearily. She was hungry, and it was growing dark.

"Excellent. Lt. Bonsu, get us something quick to eat. The rest of us are going to take this rig down, and store it aboard the Buzzard."

It was 0235 local time, the way humans reckoned time, when an exhausted Irene hit the button to close the Buzzard's back ramp. "Done. Oh, I am so tired," Irene said, resting her head against a structural rib inside the Buzzard's cargo compartment.

"Does anyone want to get something to eat?" Perkins asked, silently hoping everyone would decline her offer.

"I am too tired to eat anything, ma'am," Derek responded.

"Anyone else? No? Striebich, Bonsu, you two get some rack time. The rest of us are going to take shifts here, I'll go first."

"Ma'am?" Jesse expressed surprise.

Major Perkins rapped her knuckles on the Buzzard's skin. "We got this Buzzard and drill rig working perfectly; we are not going to risk anyone screwing with them. Until we take off in," she looked at her zPhone to check her tired mind, "one day and a wakeup, we are not letting anyone near this ship, except for this team."

Nert spoke hesitantly. "Does that include me, Major Perkins?"

There was a split second hesitation in Perkin's reply while her mind raced through the potential risks. The local Ruhar had actively been working against her team; actively trying to exclude humans from missions of any importance. "Yes, Nert, it does include you. You will take the second shift, report back here at 0330. That's human time."

"Yes, I will!" Nert exclaimed excitedly, as if he were at a fun summer camp.

"Great," Perkins had to smile at the Ruhar cadet's enthusiasm. "I will send a duty rotation to everyone, we'll all take one hour shifts. Except you, Striebich and Bonsu, you won't need to be back here until 1400."

"I don't need that long, ma'am," Irene said as she attempted to stifle a yawn.

"Yes you do," Perkins insisted. "We need the two of you to fly us, the day after tomorrow. The rest of us can sleep while you are flying."

"Yes, Major," Irene said gratefully. "I can't promise an inflight movie."

"I'll settle for peanuts," Perkins was also fighting a yawn.

"Peanuts are in short supply on this planet."

"Understood. Now get out of here."

Nert arrived fifteen minutes early for his shift as guard. "Good morning, Major Perkins," he said cheerily, not looking at all as if he had just awakened from a twenty minute nap. Ruhar, with their genetically enhanced biology, did not need as much sleep as humans did, and a short, deep nap was refreshing enough for one day. Nert would need a solid night of sleep later.

"Good morning, Cadet Dandurf. You are here early," Perkins blinked slowly to get her tired eyes to focus properly.

"I am told that your military has a saying; 'if you are not early, you are late'. It is similar in the Ruhar military."

"That is good to know, thank you."

"Do you have anything to report?" Nert asked, peering across the airbase. Pools of light from poles here and there and hangars illuminated those areas, leaving twilight in between. He swept an arc around the parked Buzzard with vision-enhancing lenses, finding only two base personnel walking toward a line of Dobrehs.

"Hmm?" Perkins forgot for a moment that she had been on guard duty. "No. People came over to speak with me twice, I did not allow them near the aircraft."

"I shall do the same. Politely, of course."

"Of course."

Nert glanced at his zPhone to check the time. It was 0322; his shift did not officially begin for another eight minutes. The human female appeared tired, although he was not an expert on human facial expressions and body language. "Major Perkins, you may be relieved," he hoped he had used the correct terminology; zPhones often could not be trusted with subtle cultural nuances. "I am sufficiently rested."

"Thank you, Nert, I will remain until 0330." Perkins did not want to appear slack in front of a Ruhar.

"Good!" Nert was delighted. "Major Perkins," he looked away, avoiding eye contact. "During the flight, I would very much like to be aboard this aircraft."

"Oh?" That surprised Perkins. All the other Ruhar would be aboard the lead Buzzard. During their joint missions to reactivate projectors, they had never had a Ruhar with them; no Ruhar wanted to ride with lowly, primitive humans. "We would be pleased to have you with us," Perkins said, instantly questioning whether she should she have said 'honored' rather than 'pleased'.

Nert made a short bow, grinning ear to ear. "Thank you, Major Perkins. As your team liaison, I believe it is proper that I remain with you."

"You will need to bring your own food supply, as well as, any, other, uh, items you may require," she stumbled awkwardly. She did not know about Ruhar sanitary habits, and even this stretched version of the Buzzard had only one cramped bathroom. The

Ruhar bunks were considered comfortably large for humans; while Nert likely would not be able to fully stretch his legs out while he slept.

"I will. This will be an adventure! I have never flown so far in a, Buz-zard," he used the unfamiliar human name for the aircraft, even knowing the name was vaguely insulting.

Great, Perkins thought to herself. We not only have a mission where our every move will be scrutinized and criticized, and now we not only will have an alien aboard for a very long flight. We will have a young, and annoyingly *enthusiastic*, alien aboard. Was there any way this mission possibly become even more wonderful?

Admiral Kekrando stood stiffly in his most formal uniform, waiting by the airlock door to the destroyer's portside docking bay. On a display mounted on the opposite wall, he could see the bay's large outer doors were open, and a sleek, dark green Jeraptha dropship was maneuvering itself into position in the docking cradle. Kekrando and a smattering of the ship's senior officers were there to greet the Jeraptha inspection team, who would be assuring all ships under Kekrando's nominal command were in compliance with their requirements for attaching to a massive yet vulnerable star carrier. Jeraptha star carriers had transported Kristang ships before, just as the Thuranin had transported Ruhar ships between the stars, but it was still an unusual and anxiety-inducing event for both sides.

The enemy dropship attached itself firmly to the cradle, and the outer door began to slide ponderously closed. Once the outer doors were securely sealed, air would be pumped into the bay, and the Jeraptha would emerge. Four minutes remaining, at least, before the patrons of the Ruhar would step through the airlock and formally onto the deck of the destroyer.

Kekrando fervently prayed for death to somehow strike him before that moment.

Beside the admiral, executive officer Kartow sweated in his own formal dress uniform, pressed in too close to the admiral in the narrow corridor. Kartow had prayed for the destroyer's captain to volunteer for the reception party, but the captain had insisted Kartow take his place; the captain was vitally needed on the bridge. The bridge of a ship hanging dead in space, with reactors shut down, and nothing for the captain to do. Kartow had done as ordered.

The discomfort of the awkward silence finally got to Kartow, and he had to say something. "Admiral, you have met the Jeraptha before? What are they like?"

"I have met them," Kekrando answered, grateful someone wished to speak with him, even though he knew the conversation was forced. What to say about the Jeraptha? That most species thought of them as insects, even though the Jeraptha had long ago lost their exoskeletons and now had a greenish, leathery outer skin? Four legs, two arms, and antennas the Jeraptha sometimes used as an extra set of fingers? No, Kartow would know all that from the clan database. "The Jeraptha appear deceptively unprofessional. They joke, and attempt to distract you. They wish you to think of them as not serious, even childish. Do not be fooled. They are a deadly enemy, with technology far beyond our capability, and even more advanced than the Thuranin." Kekrando knew that statement was considered treasonous, and it actually felt good that he no longer needed to care. His impending death was, in a way, a sort of freedom.

"I will remain focused on my duty, Admiral," Kartow replied, not knowing what else to say. To his relief, the indicator light above the airlock blinked then glowed steadily, as the bay was now fully pressurized. The enemy was coming to visit.

The airlock door slid open, and Kartow's nose detected a whiff of something sweet. Three Jeraptha came through the door. Each walked on four legs supporting a horizontal body segment, with their upper body vertical, though their heads barely came up to Kekrando's chest. They wore white and black clothing and black boots, and each of the three wore a different colored band on their left arms. The first one, with a red armband, loudly slurped from a squeeze bottle, and as it drank, it became obvious the bottle was the source of the sweet scent.

"You brought beverages with you?" Even Kekrando was surprised by that. Two of the Jeraptha appeared unsteady on their four feet, as if they had been imbibing intoxicating substances during the flight from the star carrier.

"Of course!" Blue armband said as it let out a loud belch, suddenly filling the air in the corridor with the scent of fermented, something. "This is an inspection *party*, right?"

"Oh," the Jeraptha with the yellow armband sputtered while drinking from a squeeze globe it carried in one hand, "this is the worst party *ever*. Look at all these gloomy faces! Let's get some music on." It waved the squeeze globe under Kartow's nose. "Here, drink some *burgoze*, it will put you in a better mood," it laughed.

Kartow recoiled from the stinky-smelling fluid, pressing his back against the bulkhead.

"You! You are Admiral Kekrando?" The red-banded Jeraptha gestured angrily at Kekrando, going as far as to poke the Kristang senior commander in the chest with an antenna. "You cost me a lot of money, you *chootah!*"

Kekrando stood his ground, knowing he was being baited, and suspecting the Jeraptha of being slightly drunk. Or more than slightly.

"You put that incompetent fool Gerkaw in command of your pursuit force," red-band complained as it tapped Kekrando with its antenna. "If that idiot had survived two more days, just two days, I would have won the pool! He didn't need to capture or destroy Commodore Ferlant's ships, all he needed to do was survive. For two short days. But no! He just couldn't do it, and he cost me a ton of money."

"You wagered on the outcome of the battle?" Kartow asked, incredulous.

"Of course," blue-band answered, as if it were the dumbest sort of question. "We always do, how we could we pass up juicy action like that? Don't worry about Saksey," he gestured with an antenna toward the red-banded Jeraptha, "he bet on Gerkaw to survive longer. On our ship, everyone knows," blue-band spoke in unison with yellow-band, "always bet against Saksey!" That threw blue and yellow into uproarious laughter.

"Oh, you two are *so* funny," Saksey looked at the deck while furiously sucking on his squeeze bulb, and he let out another loud, odiferous belch.

"Did anyone wager for Captain Gerkaw to succeed?" Kartow asked innocently, sparking the Jeraptha into convulsive laughter. The aliens were laughing so hard they couldn't catch their breath, and they were pounding their rear feet on the deck.

"Hahahahahahahahaha! Oh, that is a good one? Bet on Gerkaw? I would not have bet on Gerkaw to succeed against a group of Ruhar cadets. Against Commodore Ferlant?" The Jeraptha snickered. "Ha! Ferlant is a skilled and inventive commander, we have been watching his career closely and with much optimism. No," he laughed again, "not even Saksey would be dumb enough to bet on," another round of convulsive laughter, "*Gerkaw* to defeat Ferlant."

When the three Jeraptha caught their breath enough to speak, Kekrando addressed blue-band, who appeared to be the leader. At least blue-band was least unsteady on his feet. "Do you have a wager on how long I will live, once we return to the clan?" The admiral asked, almost with detached disinterest.

Trouble on Paradise

"Oh, certainly," two of the Jeraptha slapped antennas. "Not long!" Blue-band laughed. "If you want a piece of the action, you can get in-" he broke up laughing.

Saksey finished the thought. "But you won't be around to collect!"

The actual inspection was shockingly casual, with the Jeraptha poking randomly around the ship, missing vital areas and wasting time in places like the corridors near the officer's cabins. By the time the inspection was over, Saksey was swaying so badly on his feet that blue-band had to support him back to the airlock. "This has been a *terrible* party," Saksey complained with a hiccup. "Not even any snacks! We-" his thought was interrupted by another belch. "Oh, let's get out of here."

The Jeraptha were as glad to get off the Kristang destroyer as their hosts were glad to see them go. "That was a pointless exercise, Admiral," Kartow observed with disgust. "They didn't inspect anything."

"A physical inspection may not have been their purpose," Kekrando mused. "They could have scanned our ship without coming aboard."

"Then why bother coming aboard?"

"I do not know, Kartow. Perhaps they simply wished to gloat over a defeated enemy," Kekrando said, misery finally showing on his voice. "I will change out of this uniform," he looked down at his magnificent apparel. The same uniform he would wear again when he appeared before the clan leadership, in disgrace.

In his cabin, Kekrando changed out of his formal uniform, and back into a plain set of fatigues that were more appropriate for a warrior. The neck of the dress uniform must be too tight, he thought as he pulled the neckline of the fatigues away from his skin and scratched his neck. And scratched it again. It was uncomfortable, he thought of putting a cream on his neck to stop it from-

"Admiral!" The comm system in the wall console alerted him. "We have a problem!"

In the engineering control chamber of the destroyer, one of the reactor engineers was also tugging on the collar of his own formal dress uniform, which he still wore. The admiral had ordered the entire crew to dress formally to receive the Jeraptha, who had not even bothered to enter the back half of the ship! The engineering team had their bots scrubbing and cleaning and polishing every surface, even inside areas that could only be accessed by removing hatches. Bots were not good enough for some chores, the crew had gotten on hands and knees to clean and polish manually. Domestic chores such as cleaning were menial tasks for bots, slaves and females, and humiliating to any Kristang warrior. And after all the painstaking effort, wasted effort, the disgusting, arrogant Jeraptha had not looked at any of the engineering spaces. Had not even glanced at a single missile to assure its warhead detonation device had been removed.

The reactor engineer did not have much to do, as the only active reactor aboard the ship was the small auxiliary power unit. The engineering team had feared the Jeraptha would demand even that relatively weak unit be put in cold shutdown before the destroyer attached to the star carrier, leaving the entire ship relying on backup power. Fortunately, even the Jeraptha understood that the main reactors could not have their containment systems energized by backup power, and allowed the APU to remain online. That is odd, the engineer thought to himself, the console instruments indicated the APU was running slightly warm, despite the coolant system operating perfectly. Then the console shows the temperature of the reactor spiking, and the engineer sniffed the air. Smoke!

Craig Alanson

The three Jeraptha climbed up the ramp into their dropship. As soon as the ramp was securely closed, two of them dropped the pretense of being inebriated. Blue armband had to help Saksey into a seat, because Saksey, still bitter about losing the wager, had actually filled his squeeze bulb with burgoze. "That was not," Saksey hiccupped, "not as much fun as it could have been."

"Be patient, Saksey," yellow armband assured his crewmate. "I'll wager in a few minutes, you will think our little trip was well worth our time."

"Yes!" Blue armband agreed, and the two slapped antennas gleefully.

"I will not take that wager," Saksey muttered morosely. "It had better be something damned entertaining to brighten up my day." What he had not mentioned was that he had just lost another bet, a bet about the Kristang admiral's attire. Saksey had wagered the disgraced Kristang would wear regular shipboard fatigues, to show disdain for, and defiance of, the Jeraptha. He had lost, because Kekrando, indeed every crewman aboard the destroyer, had been wearing full dress uniform.

The dropship was less than halfway back to the star carrier, when they received notice of a potentially serious problem aboard the Kristang flagship. Fire in an auxiliary reactor, the destroyer was preparing to maneuver and possibly eject the reactor core from the ship; all ships in the area were warned to avoid a radioactive explosion. To the confusion of Saksey, his companions were chuckling, then laughing uncontrollably. "We had better," yellow armband said between gales of laughter, "tell them before they really do eject it."

"What did you do?" Saksey asked, checking that he was securely held in the seat in case the dropship had to perform emergency maneuvers.

"An old classic, Saksey! Sometimes the best tricks are the simple ones. Smoke bomb in the reactor compartment! We dropped nanobots that crawled through their ventilation system to their engineering spaces. By now, they think the auxiliary reactor is overheating, and the compartment should be filled with smoke. Oh, I wish I could see their ugly faces when they realize it is only a simple smoke bomb!"

Saksey chuckled also, he had to admit that was a good one. "I am glad I did not take your wager. I love messing with the Kristang, they are so gullible."

"Wait," blue armband struggled to say, he was laughing so hard, "wait until the admiral discovers the itching powder in his uniform fatigues. Another oldie but goodie! I tell you, when messing with a low-tech species, simple tricks are the best."

Admiral Kekrando received an all-clear from the destroyer's captain, who was chagrinned to admit the problem had been only a smoke bomb. A simple practical joke that had the destroyer's crew less than thirty seconds from ejecting the reactor core, before an engineer discovered the smoke-generating device behind a pipe.

Admiral Kekrando's acknowledgement was delayed, as he was in the shower, furiously scrubbing his itching skin. And hoping, whatever else fate had in store for him, that he never again had to deal with the Jeraptha.

39 Commando's Jawkuar completed its long flight, and the pilots set it down as close to the objective as possible. The wings of the Jawkuar bent or broke tree branches, and the belly of the dropship flattened one small tree and several shrubs; that could not be prevented. The commando leader was the first to pop the door open and breath in blessedly fresh air, filling his lungs in great, greedy gulps. To enhance stealth, the air circulation inside the Jawkuar had been kept at a minimum, and the air in the cabin had been stale and increasingly thick with the stink of unwashed Kristang warriors. The

Trouble on Paradise

commando leader walked down the steps onto the stony, sandy soil; his boots crunched on dried leaf litter from the palm trees which swayed in the steady trade winds.

His second in command walked down to stand beside him. "Ah, that air is a relief. It's too bad we're here on a mission; this island would be a pleasant place to relax."

"Relax? Without females to serve us?" The leader scoffed, but winked at his second. "It is nice," he said, enjoying the hot sun on his skin. "I will have to remember this place, after we take this planet back from the Ruhar."

"If we are successful," the second chuckled, "this island won't be here."

"True." Then the leader snapped out of his brief tropical reverie. "Stealth netting goes up first, then set up jammers and repeaters. Get those trees," he pointed to the branches broken by the Jawkuar's descent, "trimmed, and bend some of these palms down to lean over the ship." The palms were tall enough. "I'm going to inspect the site." He scuffed away soil with the heel of his boot. "Perhaps fortune will smile on us, and this will be easy."

"This is a volcanic island," the second repeated data from the geological survey. "It could be all hardened lava under this sand."

"If it is," the leader said sourly, "I will blame your negative thoughts."

CHAPTER EIGHT

"Got it! Trace reacquired," the *Mem Hertall*'s sensor technician muttered excitedly. He was too tired to shout, having been awake almost continuously while his ship tracked the extremely faint particle trail left by what he was certain was the Kristang frigate *To Seek Glory in Battle is Glorious*. "Tagging location. Bring us about again," he advised the duty officer, "we need to triangulate the trace."

"Bring us about, *again*," the duty officer wearily ordered the ship's helmsman. Again. How many times had they done that already? She could not remember. Even the ship's computer may have lost track of how many times they had performed the same, repetitive action.

Knowing the duty officer, and the entire crew, were bored out of their minds, the sensor tech stood up, stretched, then announced "Particle density was up another eighteen percent that time. We're closing."

The duty officer rose from her chair excitedly. "You are sure?"

The tech pointed to the display. "See for yourself, Ma'am."

"How close?" The *Hertall* had been coordinating the search with the *Toman* and the *Grathur*. Each of the three ships wanted to do everything they could to find a dangerous enemy. And the crew of each ship wanted their own ship to be the one who found the *Glory*. So far, the *Mem Hertall* was significantly in the lead.

The tech rubbed the back of his aching neck. "Close. With this level of particle density, that ship must have significant battle damage. She is spewing out reactor coolant, she has a leaky airlock, and her hull coating is flaking off. From the hull coating alone, the database can be certain we're tracking our old friend the *Glory*."

"Close, like?" The duty officer asked anxiously. The ship was now only on yellow alert, the highest condition of combat readiness that could be sustained for a long period. If combat was imminent, she should take the ship to red alert. Or Captain Rastall, who was sleeping in his cabin next to the bridge, should do that. "Should I notify the captain?"

The sensor tech held up a finger for quiet, as the *Hertall* crossed the trace cloud from a different direction. "Got it. Up twenty two percent, and the trail is straight as an arrow. *Now*, you should wake up the captain."

The Kristang Special Forces warriors of 39 Commando prepared a stealth communications drone. Folded up for deployment, the device was no larger than a walnut shell, but surprisingly heavy as it consisted of tightly packed nanomaterial. The Kristang special forces were in luck that day, or they had been smart enough to wait for the afternoon trade winds to pick up, for a stiff and steady breeze blew out of the west. To launch the stealth drone, two Kristang handled a thin tube that extended out to ten meters' length. A magnetic impulse launched the walnut, which grew guidance fins after it left the launch tube. When it reached peak altitude at eighteen hundred meters and began to fall, the fins retracted and the outer shell exploded away, revealing a gossamer-thin parachute. At the center of the steerable parachute, the communications drone was a now the size of a lima bean, and encased in a fuzzy stealth field. To wrap even such a tiny object in stealth took enormous power, and the drone's life was limited to thirteen hours. That was much more time than needed, if nothing went drastically wrong.

The brain of the drone steered the parachute to catch uplifting winds, and avoid downdrafts. It was carried far from the island, climbing higher and higher on soaring thermals, until it reached the point where the air was too thin to provide additional lift. At that point, the parachute material reformed itself into a tall, thin balloon, and the drone filled the balloon with heated hydrogen gas. It climbed rapidly, then its ascent slowed, with the balloon's envelope expanding as the atmosphere fell away. When the drone judged it could rise no higher, it squirted its message into space on a laser beam with less than two milliseconds duration. Then the drone self-destructed gently into a fine powder. It would take the powder months to fall to the surface, far across the surface of the ocean.

Because the laser beam was initiated so high above the surface, there were few atmospheric particles to create backscatter. Sensors on a Ruhar satellite detected only the faintest trace of a signal, which the sensor network dismissed as most likely being caused by a cosmic ray or micrometeorite.

The laser beam, in the vacuum of space, travelled outward on its lonely journey, encountering only the occasional particle propelled by the solar wind of Paradise's star. Thirty minutes later, the beam's strength was still 86% of its original power, well above the 22% needed to be successfully read by a Kristang frigate.

The battered and overworked little frigate *Glory* had been loitering at the signal rendezvous point, thirty lightminutes from the planet the Kristang knew as Pradassis. The hair-thin laser beam was intercepted by the frigate's extended sensor field, causing that ship's captain to congratulate his navigator's precision. If their position in deep space had been off by as little as the height of a Kristang warrior, they would have missed the signal. The captain privately thought their ability to intercept the signal was a miracle, or luck, rather than precision.

The *Glory*'s captain read the message and frowned. The ship's second in command read the message and groaned. "Sir," the second officer protested quietly, "this will require extremely precise timing. And navigation. To jump into an area this small?" He meant the small sphere of space above Pradassis where the *Glory* was supposed to rendezvous with the Jawkuar dropship of 39 Commando. "With the poor condition of our jump drive, we would need to jump in close to the planet, then make a second, short jump to the rendezvous point. That is the only way we could have hope of jumping into an area this precise."

The captain clapped his second officer on the back with hearty Kristang warrior slap. "Ha! You joke, Smando. This ship's obsolete jump drive could not bring us into these coordinates if we were already there. *Krell*," he used a Kristang curse word, "we will be lucky not to emerge from jump inside the damned planet. No matter," he sighed, "we have our orders. At least we know where and when this mission will end, one way or another."

"Captain," Second Officer Smando said with a forced smile. Sometimes his captain's gallows humor was too much to take. "We will need to hit the rendezvous with a second jump. We will lose the advantage of surprise. 39 Commando will need to fly their Jawkuar directly into our landing bay without delay; we have to jump away within forty seconds."

"Forty?" The captain raised a skeptical eyebrow. "Thirty seconds, I think. The Ruhar sensor network is still only partly established around Pradassis, but from what little we have been able to observe, their response time is impressive."

"Thirty seconds?" Smando clenched his teeth. That was impossibly quick.

"Do not worry, Smando," the captain pounded his underling on the back again. "I have some ideas on how to buy us time. Enough time? Perhaps not. Ah, this ship has tempted fate far too many times already. At this point, the suspense of not knowing when we will die is killing me. Better to get it over with, eh?"

Smando's lips twisted into a weak grin. "Yes, sir." He wondered again, for the thousandth time, why he had not taken his father's advice and requested a nice shore assignment. To seek glory in battle was indeed glorious; it was also dangerous. If he somehow survived his term of service aboard the *Glory*, he would put his career ambitions aside for a time and simply enjoy being alive. If he lived that long.

It was a long, long flight, mostly over water. The flight was tiring for Irene and Derek, mostly because their flying was constantly criticized by the Ruhar pilots who were flying the lead Buzzard. The criticism was particularly annoying, because for most of the flight, the humans had their Buzzard on autopilot, guided by signals from the lead ship.

"*Toonal*, fall back 2.27 kilometers, you are crowding me," called the Ruhar pilot in the lead ship. "And you are low, climb eighteen hundred meters to the glidepath."

"Asshole," Irene muttered under her breath and pointed to the main cockpit display that was projected onto the windshield. "We are exactly on the freakin' glidepath! And point eight kilometers' separation is textbook flight procedure, for a two-ship formation at this speed and altitude."

Derek knew nothing he said would soothe his pilot's anger; he said it anyway. "He's not unhappy with your flying, he objects that we are humans. Nothing we do will be good enough for him." Fortunately, the Buzzard had plenty of fuel to reach the island, with a comfortable safety margin. They would not need to perform inflight refueling until the flight back. At that point in the mission, the giant maser projector would be online, and no one would care how skillfully the humans performed on the return flight. After drilling down to the projector control chamber, there wouldn't be much for the humans to do. Derek was hoping they would find time to relax on one of the beautiful white sand beaches of the island, and go swimming. He had researched whether swimming in the oceans of Paradise was safe, because there were predators in the water. Each of the humans had a Ruhar device they could wear around their waists that would deter predators, and Nert assured him he was looking forward to swimming. Derek was looking forward to seeing Irene in a bikini. Or less.

Irene cocked her head at her copilot, for him having stated the obvious. "Yeah, like I said, he's an asshole." She keyed the console to respond. "Understood, *Kiwi*, will comply." She pulled back on the yoke to initiate a climb.

"The lead pilot's callsign is *Kliwa*, not *Kiwi*," Nert chided her gently from the jumpseat behind her.

"The callsign they gave us is *Toonal*, that is the baby chick of a bird known for flying awkwardly on your home planet, right?" Irene asked without turning to look at their 'liaison officer'.

"Yes, that is unfortun- Oh, ha, ha, the translator explained to me that a Kiwi is an Earth bird that is incapable of flying," Nert giggled. "That is funny."

"Uh, yes," Irene regretted being flippant. This mission wasn't about reactivating another projector, it was about building trust with the Ruhar. Insulting a Ruhar pilot was not a tactic likely to build a positive relationship. "I shouldn't have said that, sorry."

"There is no need to be sorry, Lieutenant Striebich," Nert giggled again. "He did indeed insult you with that callsign, you are right to give it right back to him. As you stated, he is an asshole. The next time you speak with him, tell him 'fuck you very much'," Nert said with a jaw-stretching grin.

Irene and Derek couldn't help laughing. It was good to see their young liaison officer had a healthy sense of humor about himself. Against her better judgment, Irene pulled back on the control stick to initiate a climb, pulling her Buzzard higher and far behind the lead ship. The Ruhar wanted space to fly? Fine, Irene would give it to him. She waited until she was ten kilometers behind and a thousand meters higher; the Ruhar pilot did not object, or he didn't care.

"There it is," Derek called excitedly from the right-hand seat, sitting up straight in his seat and craning his neck to see over the console. He toggled the intercom open. "The island is dead ahead of us, if anyone wants a view. We're passing a chain of similar islands to our right." The islands were even more beautiful than they appeared in pictures. Lush, tropical peaks surrounded with white sand beaches, brilliantly blue water and fringing reefs. Derek couldn't wait to get the drilling over with and hit the beach.

"*Toonal*, orbit here while I circle the island and select two landing areas," the lead pilot ordered.

"Understood, *Kiwi*," Irene said with a tight smile, pulling the Buzzard into a tight turn, so she was flying circles over a peninsula that stuck out like a finger into the azure water. "The landing area for my ship need clearance for us to unload the drill rig." The lead pilot could land in a clearing barely large enough for his ship, and he probably would do that to show off. Irene required space to get the drill rig out the back ramp, and attach it to the sling so she could carry it to the projector site.

"I know that, *Toonal*," the Ruhar snapped, irritated.

"He's jealous that he doesn't have the skill to hover with the drill rig in a sling," Irene muttered to Derek.

"That's going to be tricky in this wind," Derek observed unhappily, watching the palm trees ripple and sway in the strong winds. "I'm reading the wind fluctuating between eight and ten meters per second."

"Compared to the katabatic wind on our first arctic mission, that's nothing."

"On this mission, we don't have any margin for error," Derek reminded his fellow pilot. They were not only too far away to quickly get spare parts if they broke anything. Major Perkins had explained in confidence to her pilots that this could very well be humanity's last mission for the Ruhar. They absolutely could not afford to screw anything up.

"Yeah, yeah," Irene waved a hand dismissively. "We'll use a guide cable anchored to the ground, and winch the rig down. Piece of cake. Asshole up there is going to be disappointed if he is hoping to watch us make a mistake," Irene flipped a middle finger toward the windscreen, at the lead ship.

"Lieutenant Striebich, you feel strong romantic affection for the lead pilot?" Nert expressed surprise from the jump seat behind Irene.

"What? For that jerk?" She turned in her seat to glance at their liaison officer. "No!"

"But," Nert sputtered, confused. "You made a gesture to initiate mating?"

"I did n-"

Nert continued. "Is not your middle finger a human gesture meaning 'fuck you'?"

"Oh God," Derek broke into laughter, as Irene's face grew beet red. "He is right, Irene. You're sweet on your Kiwi boy up there?"

"I am n-" She never finished.

Derek held up a hand. "I just lost external sensors," he reported with alarm. "I can't see the lead ship with the sensor field. And," he looked at Irene, eyes wide open. "We lost satellite guidance. We're not receiving the navigation signals."

"Is it us? We're not receiving *anything*." Irene scanned the console, seeking sign of a problem with the Buzzard's antennas. "I don't see any-"

Ahead of them, over the center peak of the island, a bright burning streak shot up from the tree cover, striking the lead ship in the belly, directly below where the wings attached. The Ruhar's Buzzard blew apart in an orange fireball, pieces raining down widely over the island.

Irene reacted instantly, throwing her Buzzard into a full power dive. The cockpit computer's Bitchin' Betty was shouting warnings at her. Usually the computer-generated voice called out semi-useful alerts like 'Terrain! Pull up!' or 'Power loss in starboard engine'. This time the voice was shouting a 'Missile Inbound' warning that Irene found completely freakin' obvious, so she ignored it. "Hang on back there," she said into the intercom, "this is going to get kinetic in a hurry." Derek's teamwork was perfect; he engaged the ship's stealth field, antimissile active countermeasures and defensive maser turrets. Those actions, and their distance from the mountain peak where 39 Commando was hiding, were almost enough.

Almost.

Irene chopped power and flared to avoid smacking into the surface of the sea, intending to hug the tree cover of the shoreline until the highest mountain peak was masked by the smaller peak of the island. The Buzzard roared just above the waves, no more than twenty meters from the beach, when Derek called out a warning. "Three missiles inbound!"

Irene pulled the Buzzard toward the beach, racing barely above the waves. She slammed the engines into full reverse and the Buzzard stood on its nose, before swinging the engines quickly back down into a hover. With both engines scouring sand off the beach, she tucked the aircraft between tall palms trees to slide to a rough landing, the skids gouging long furrows in the sparklingly white sand. If they got hit, she did not want to be moving fast or over water. Best to be on the ground, where the enemy missiles' sensors might be confused by ground clutter. And maneuvering the awkward, lumbering transport aircraft at low speed was useless against missiles.

The stealth and countermeasures either worked or they did not.

They almost did.

One missile got confused by ripples in the sea surface where the Buzzard's belly jets had disturbed the water. That missile impacted the surface, plunged into the sandy bottom and exploded, throwing a fountain of sand, mud, salt water and sea creatures skyward.

The second missile slowed its approach to evaluate the cloud of water spray thrown up by the first missile. Its hesitation gave the Buzzard's defensive maser turrets time to lock on, and two turrets combined to burn through the nose of the missile, frying its brain and rendering it inert. That missile continued forward on momentum alone, crashing through trees a half kilometer beyond the motionless Buzzard.

Unfortunately, the third missile detected the defensive maser fire, and homed in on that location. The maser turrets switched their focus to the third missile, hindered by that missile approaching from an angle where one turret couldn't fire as it was behind the Buzzard's tail. The third missile was exploded by a maser beam, eighty meters from the Buzzard. The high-velocity shape charge of warhead shrapnel struck the Buzzard, tearing into one idling engine, and hot chunks of debris peppered the fuselage.

"Damage report," Major Perkins shouted, once pieces of hot shrapnel had stopped bouncing about the cabin.

"Starboard engine took a hit, I don't know how bad yet," Irene reported from the cockpit. "It shut down automatically before it tore itself apart. We're got damage to multiple flight control systems, uh, a couple powercells." She looked back at Perkins. "The starboard engine is the big problem, it's probably scrap. I won't know until I can look inside."

Trouble on Paradise

That wasn't great, it also wasn't the total disaster Perkins had feared. "Is anyone injured?"

No one had any injury worse than minor cuts from flying shrapnel; they had been saved by the armor around the passenger cabin. "Everyone out!" Perkins ordered, worried there might be another missile on its way to them.

Hearing Major Perkins' order to abandon ship, Irene moved as quickly as she could, given the somewhat awkward seat release mechanism that was designed for larger Ruhar bodies. She had complained several times about the compromised ergonomics of the Buzzard cockpit setup, and now one item had the potential to kill her. She got the straps released, and the side bolsters of the seat automatically slid down, with the center control stand between the seats retracting forward to clear a path for her and Derek. That was all great and much better than any human-built mechanism could have done. The problem was the nanofabric parachute that the entire team wore as a fannypack around their waists. The Ruhar parachute was incredible technology, able to protect the wearer in a high-speed bailout. The parachute's computer was smart enough to adjust to the generally smaller size of humans, even Irene's petite frame. She still had the issue of the parachute's strap being too long, so that when she had the damned thing properly cinched around her waist, a loop hung down, creating a snag hazard that would never be allowed for a Ruhar pilot. Irene had suggested trimming the excess material, but the loop was integral to the nanofabric storage, so the Ruhar had not allowed that.

Now the loop was snagged on part of the central control stand, trapping her. With a lack of patience that would surprise no one with knew her, she yanked her combat knife out of a boot and sawed through the tough nanofabric with the blade she always kept razor sharp. It felt good to finally be rid of that annoyance. "Let's go!" She ordered Derek, who had been waiting for her anxiously, his own knife ready to assist.

They ran away from the Buzzard, stumbling over rocks and tree roots into the forest, headed for higher ground. A thin trail of gray smoke rose from the stricken engine, wafting barely above the treetops before being carried away by the steady trade winds. "Ten minutes should do it, Ma'am," Irene advised. "If they don't attack again in ten minutes, they think we're already dead."

"Three missiles were fired at us," Nert said through the zPhone translator, which always made the young cadet sound older. "We should be dead. Lt. Striebich, that was smart to land the aircraft; that is not a technique in our flight training. You saved our lives," his face reflected admiration.

Irene looked at the ground, embarrassed by the praise. "I figured we had zero chance in the air, and if we got hit, I'd rather already be on the ground. I wish we'd had time to evac before that last missile hit."

"I don't think so," Jesse used a knife to dig a still-warm piece of shrapnel out of a palm tree trunk. He held the jagged fragment up for the others to see. "I wouldn't want to be out here when that warhead exploded. The Buzzard's cabin is armored."

"Specialist Colter is correct," Nert agreed with the overbite expression that was the Ruhar version of a frown.

"Why here?" Shauna shook her head, dazed. Minutes ago, she had been looking forward to swimming in the spectacularly aquamarine waters. Wearing a bikini for the first time in many months. Relaxing in the tropical sunshine. Maybe finding a secluded beach where she and Jesse would have some private fun.

"Yeah, what the hell happened?" Dave's mind was still reeling.

"Striebich, what's the POO for those missiles?" Perkins asked about the Point Of Origin.

"Just below the highest peak, Ma'am," Irene reported. "They were all toggled off from the same area."

"Whoever they are, they're here for the maser projector, then," Perkins declared, a hand flying to her mouth as she realized the full horror of the situation. "The question is not *why* or *what*," Perkins announced. "The question is *when*? Why now?"

Nert gasped and finished her thought for her. "The transports!"

"Two Ruhar transport ships jumped into orbit early yesterday," Perkins explained. "The Kristang must be working to get this projector operational so they can use it against those ships." How the fuck, Perkins thought, had Ruhar intelligence missed a Kristang combat team? A team capable of flying across the ocean, a team large and well-equipped enough to attempt to dig down and reactivate a maser projector. The official intelligence reports the Ruhar had shared with UNEF HQ stated emphatically that every single Kristang had been evacuated off the surface. RUMINT, the unofficial rumor intelligence of gossip, had been going around for weeks that the Ruhar military was chasing ghosts around the planet; looking for a Kristang commando unit. The Ruhar had flatly denied any such rumors, but now Emily Perkins had a breaking news flash for them; the Kristang were still on Paradise, and still dangerous.

"The transports arrived yesterday, and the Kristang haven't shot at them," Derek noted. "The Kristang haven't been able to get the projector working yet?"

"How many people are aboard those transports?" Shauna asked.

"Thirty nine thousand eight hundred and sixty four!" Nert shouted through the translator, with the device being annoyingly precise as usual. "We must warn them!"

"I tried that already," Perkins held up her zPhone. "The island is under a stealth field, and they're jamming all outbound signals."

"I tried the comm system in the Buzzard," Irene shook her head. "Nothing's going out."

"The Ruhar must have seen the crash, right?" Jesse suggested. "Or, hey, the Ruhar will know something is wrong when we don't report in."

Major Perkins shook her head. "Good thinking, but the Kristang will have picked up our transmissions on the way in, and they'll be mimicking our signals. No one outside will know anything is wrong here until it's too late." She wondered what type of Kristang unit they had stumbled across. Whoever they were, they had to be pissed off that a pair of Buzzards had flown out of nowhere and almost landed in their laps. Antiaircraft missiles, a stealth field powerful enough to cover an island and beyond, jammers, signal maskers, and some sort of gear for excavating down to a projector and taking control of it. This was no amateur group of Kristang who had lingered behind and hidden during the evacuation. Perkins realized her team was facing a determined and capable adversary. And her team had not a single weapon between them, not even Nert.

Nert held Perkins' forearm and pleaded with her in plain English, using his halting knowledge of the language. "You need stop Kristang!"

"I would like to, Nert," she squeezed his hand reassuringly. "We do not have any weapons to fight them with." To her team, she shook her head. "This is one hell of a soup sandwich, people; we are black on everything useful." It was impossible to make a sandwich out of soup, although that task might be easier than attacking Kristang, without using any weapons.

Shauna and Dave looked at each other at the same time. "We do have a weapon," Shauna said with confidence. "The drill rig, Ma'am," she explained.

"How's that, Jarrett?" Perkins asked.

Trouble on Paradise

"The Kristang, whoever they are, have been digging down to reactivate this projector, right? Somehow, they would have dug, or drilled, down from the top, the shortest distance. They only need access to the control center. But we have a real drill rig," she regarded her toy with affection.

"Why would we drill down to the control center, if the Kristang already have access to it?" Derek asked, puzzled. "They must have access by now, if they're going to hit transport ships in a few hours." Derek assumed the Kristang would act before the transport ships docked with the top of the space elevator and began unloading passengers. The space station at the top of the elevator was almost over the horizon from the island, it would be a difficult shot for the projector. It would be more effective for the Kristang to hit the two ships while they were maneuvering overhead.

"We're not going to the control center. Look," Shauna pulled up a schematic of a maser projector on her zPhone. "At the base of every projector are powercells. Big banks of powercells, loaded with energy. If we use the smallest drill bit," she opened her palm to show a drill bit thinner than a pencil. "We can reach those powercells."

"Won't the Kristang figure out what we're doing, and stop us? We'll have to set up the drill rig close to them," Perkins worried.

"No, Ma'am, we won't," Jesse was bursting with enthusiasm for Shauna's idea. "Shauna is right. We don't have to drill only vertically; this thing can drill a horizontal bore. It can even drill upward; we can steer the drill bit. We can't do it from way out here," Jesse looked around.

"No," Shauna agreed. "We will need to get the rig closer. But, Ma'am, the Kristang won't know what we're doing, until the drill bit gets close to the powercells. When they do," she frowned, "we'll need to be ready for them."

"All right," Perkins considered the idea. "You can knock the powercells offline, by drilling into them?"

"No, Ma'am, there's too many of them, and they're in clusters around the base of the maser projector. Even one bank of powercells is enough for a maser shot, we would need to take all of them offline," Shauna explained. "But what we can do is cause a bank of powercells to overload and rupture. We can kluge together a surge inducer. I know how to do that," she added with an ironic grin, "because that is in the big list of things Emby warned us not to do around a projector."

"An overload could destroy the projector?" Perkins asked hopefully.

Shauna grimaced. "That could destroy this whole island. The explosion of one bank would trigger release of energy from the entire array. That is, according to one of the Ruhar I talked with on our last mission."

"That is not optimal for us," Perkins stated the obvious.

Shauna held up her hands. "It's an all or nothing thing, Ma'am. Once one cell overloads, all that stored energy has to go somewhere; it will rupture the other banks of cells."

Perkins considered the entire island erupting in a ginormous explosion. "Ah, the good news is we don't have to worry about target identification; if it's on this island and it's not us, we can light it up. I would rather not get blown up with the lizards."

"Once we reach the powercells with the drill bit, we could set the surge inducer to trigger later," Jesse suggested. "Set it on a timer, give us time to get away?"

"To where?" Dave swung his arms around. "We're on an island."

"There are other islands around here," Jesse pointed to the sea, where islands dotted the horizon. "We can use the emergency inflatable boats from the Buzzard, head for another island?"

Craig Alanson

Perkins rubbed the back of her neck. "If this island blows up, it will create a tsunami."

Irene pursed her lips in thought. "That's still better than being here. The boats have electric motors, we could get to one of those islands, go on the other side, or climb high enough to be clear of a tsunami. Unless someone has a better idea?"

No one did. "Jarrett," Perkins pulled out her own zPhone. Annoyingly, it still had no connection to the outside world, but the map function still worked. And she had stored extensive data about the island, especially its subsurface geology. "Show me where we need to put the drill rig, in order to reach the powercells. This discussion is academic, unless we can get the drill rig in place. There are no roads on this island."

Shauna huddled with Dave and Jesse to find a place they could drive the drill, from their current location. Irene had rejected any possibility the Buzzard could move the drill rig anywhere. Even if the Buzzard by some miracle could get in the air, no way could it hover with the drill rig suspended on a sling below. The only way they could move anywhere was for the drill rig to move on its own six articulated legs. "Here, Ma'am," Shauna announced after ten fevered minutes of searching for a location the drill rig could walk to, that also was close enough to the powercells. "We should be able to walk the drill rig up this riverbed, the tree cover is thinner there."

Perkins raised her eyebrows. "You can drill all the way to the powercells from that spot?" The projector was built into the extinct volcano that was the tallest mountain on the island. From the location Shauna had selected, they would be drilling mostly horizontally into the base of the mountain.

"Yes," Shauna nodded confidently. "According to the specs in the manual, we can easily reach the powercells from that location. The nanomaterial of the drill pipes can stretch a lot; we'll be drilling a very small diameter hole, so we have plenty of material. And with a small drill bit, we can go fast."

"You trust the manual?" Perkins was skeptical. They were dealing with extremely advanced alien technology, but she could not imagine their portable drill rig punching such a long distance through the volcanic rock of the island.

"It's been right about everything so far, Ma'am. There are a couple possible locations, I suggest we go to this site, because there's a seam of softer rock part of the way. We can drill faster there, and the vibration won't transmit as far."

Perkins examined the data. "Is there really a seam, or is that an illusion created by the projector's stealth field?" The network of projectors had remained hidden for centuries, because each projector was encased in a stealth field that fooled scanners. Instead of sensors seeing a giant machine beneath the surface, sensors had seen uninteresting dirt or rock, or whatever had been at that site, before the Kristang dug it out to install a projector.

"I don't know," Shauna hesitated, unsure. "I'm not a geologist, Ma'am," she admitted.

"That's all right, Jarrett, I'm not one either," Perkins said. "This seam does look like it runs right up to the surface. If it's there when we get there, we can assume it goes deeper. Ok, I'm sold. Get the drill rig out of the Buzzard, and make it mobile." She contemplated the map on her zPhone. "We've never walked a drill rig that far."

"No, Ma'am," Shauna agreed. "Because we're only going to drill a really narrow hole, we can leave a lot of the heavier components here. That will help it walk through the rough terrain here. We can make it."

"All right, it's been ten minutes," Perkins declared. "Back to Buzzard, we've got a hell of a lot of work to do, fast."

Trouble on Paradise

While they worked to get the drill rig unstrapped, out of the Buzzard, set up and tested, Perkins mulled over a problem in her mind. "Striebich, Bonsu, we may need your bird to make a short flight."

Irene looked shocked. Surely Major Perkins could see the damage to the aircraft. "That would be *very* short, Ma'am. I don't think it could reach the water from here. What kind of flight are you planning?"

Perkins turned to Shauna, the team's de facto drill rig 'expert'. "Jarrett, you said that if we are able to drill into the powercells, the Kristang at some point will know what we're doing?"

"Yes. Projectors have sensors in the soil around them, to detect intrusions and problems like water seepage. It depends on how well the surrounding soil transmits vibration from our drill bit. My guess is the Kristang will know something is wrong once we're within fifty meters of the powercells."

"At that point, the Kristang will come looking for us, and blow up the drill rig," Perkins declared.

"You think they can get to the drill rig that quickly, Ma'am?" Dave asked. "Kristang can move fast, sure-"

"What I *think* is," Perkins explained, "that they have an aircraft stashed around here somewhere. They sure didn't swim all the way here. I suspect they haven't used their aircraft against us yet, because they think they shot us down and we're out of the fight. There's no reason for them to risk their aircraft, and they don't know we don't have antiaircraft missiles with us." Or any weapons of any kind, Perkins thought bitterly. "You can be sure that when the Kristang figure out we're trying to blow the projector's powercells, their aircraft will be all over us. We need to find it first, and take it out."

"Our Buzzard doesn't have any weapons, Ma'am," Irene reminded her commanding officer. The defensive maser turrets didn't count; they could only be used against missiles that threatened the Buzzard.

"If it falls out of the sky onto the enemy, our Buzzard *is* a weapon," Perkins said with a smile.

"Oh," Irene was crestfallen. The Ruhar trusted her with a special aircraft, and she had already gotten it shot up. Now she was supposed to deliberately crash it?

"You can fly it remotely, correct?" Perkins knew the answer was yes.

"We can *control* it remotely," Irene answered unhappily. "This engine won't fly at all," Irene protested while pointing to the shrapnel-pockmarked starboard engine nacelle, with Derek nodding agreement. "We can draw power from the other engine, but this engine can't provide lift or thrust. There are fan blades missing, or bent." She tapped the engine cowling.

Dave hopped up to grab the lip of the intake cowling. He slipped the first time, then got a firm hold the second time. He could see what the pilots meant, many of the fan blades were a mess. "Lt. Striebich, how many fan blades do you need to take off with?"

"I'm not sure," Irene glanced to Derek. That data was probably something they could calculate, using the Buzzard's pilot manual.

"We only need a short flight, I think?" Dave asked. "These bent fan blades, I'm pretty sure I can cut them away," he offered hopefully.

Derek looked to Irene, considering the idea. "Whatever blades are left, they'll need to be balanced."

"Balanced enough," Irene mused, reluctantly warming to the idea of her precious aircraft flying one last mission. "It will only be a short flight, like he said. We can deal with vibration; we'll override the safeties."

"Flying the ship remotely, we won't get any seat of the pants feedback. I could set up a vibration sensor," Derek offered.

Irene tilted her head, amused. "Derek, I don't need my backside vibrating to fly a Buzzard. Major," she turned to Perkins. "I think it's worth a shot. If we can't get the engine balanced, we don't lose anything."

"Except time and effort," Perkins reflected unhappily. "Czajka, I appreciate the offer to work on the engine, but we need you on the drill, if we're going to get it running."

"We," Derek pointed to himself and Irene, "can handle cutting away the busted fan blades." Derek didn't want to trust a non-pilot to do that task anyway.

Irene and Derek were cutting away fan blades and testing the starboard engine, which was still vibrating terribly even at idle. Shauna, Jesse and Dave had taken the stripped-down drill rig on a long walk, first along the beach, then up a streambed into the interior of the island. The rig had sustained damage from the Kristang missile, but Shauna knew it was still functional. Emily Perkins was not a pilot, or aircraft mechanic, or familiar with the operation of the drill rig. She did have a long career as an intelligence analyst, before Emby enlisted her into reactivating centuries-old alien hyperweapons. Using her experience as an analyst, she reviewed sensor data and images collected by the Buzzard on their brief flight over the island, searching for a hidden Kristang aircraft. The enemy aircraft was almost certainly enveloped in a stealth field, a fact she confirmed by the simple reason that no aircraft was visible anywhere on the island. Between images from their own Buzzard, and those transmitted through datalink from the lead ship before it was destroyed, she could see nearly ninety percent of the island. The images and sensor data covered a hundred percent of the mountain with the buried projector, and she concentrated her search there. The Kristang would have sought a landing site as close to the projector as possible, to minimize the distance they had to carry whatever equipment they used to dig down to the projector control chamber. Perkins felt it safe to assume the Kristang, whoever they were, did not just happen to carry a portable drill rig with them. However they were getting access to the projector control chamber, they were very likely doing it with improvised equipment. Lasers, even explosive shape charges. That meant a lot of heat being generated, yet the two Buzzards had not detected anything unusual during the flight in. Or had they? Damn it! Yes, they had, Perkins saw! The Kristang no doubt had camouflage netting and a stealth field concealing the site they were excavating, and halted activity when they detected the Buzzards approaching. The Buzzards had shared a datalink, and the pilots had been communicating frequently, making it easy for the Kristang to detect them long before they approached the island. The warning the Kristang had received had been enough time for the excess heat to dissipate, and most of the remaining heat had been masked by the stealth field. Yet sensors on the Buzzards had noticed a heat signature, which had been tagged as nothing unusual on a volcano. If the crews had been paying attention, they might have asked why an extinct volcano was generating heat. Perkins did not fault her crew or the Ruhar; this part of the planet was poorly surveyed, being so far from civilization. It was an understandable mistake, though a fatal one.

Ok. So now she knew where the Kristang had a stealth field operational, that meant she could examine the characteristics of their stealth field. And look for another stealth field, somewhere near the projector.

Great idea, except it didn't work. With the sensor data she had access to, she couldn't find anything. Nothing, Nada. Zilch.

Trouble on Paradise

Fine. Forget about fancy alien technology, she would go back to basic techniques. The Kristang needed a place to land their aircraft. She looked for clearings near the projector excavation site, moving outward in circles. There were only four clearings large enough to land a Buzzard-sized aircraft within two kilometers of the projector.

Damn it! None of the four sites showed any sign of anything concealed under netting and inside a stealth field. Which was not surprising; that was the point of camouflage netting and stealth fields.

Hmmm. None of the four sites were comfortably large enough to land a Buzzard with much clearance for safety. Perkins knew her two pilots would confidently tell her they could easily set a Buzzard down with mere inches to spare; the Kristang pilots were at least as skilled. However, no pilot could prevent downwash from the jets from disturbing the surrounding trees.

Aha! "Got you, you bastard," she muttered delightedly. The largest of the four clearings, the one second closest to the projector site, had tree limbs that were limp and turning brown. They must have been broken by the aircraft as it landed. As Perkins examined the images, she whistled. "Must be a *big* sucker." Based on the sizable area of disturbed vegetation, the Kristang's aircraft was much larger than a Buzzard. Possibly some type of dropship? An interesting fact, but not relevant. She didn't need to know what type of ship the Kristang had, all she needed was to kill it.

"Got it! Striebich, Bonsu, we have a target," she announced excitedly.

"Just a minute, Ma'am," Irene's voice grunted with strain. "We just about have this-Ow! Shit! I bashed my fingers!"

"You all right?" Derek asked with concern.

"Yeah, I'm fine," Irene said, sucking on her bruises fingers. "That was stupid. Ok, that's the last one, let's try it again." She dropped to the ground and backed away from the engine. "Major Perkins, it's best if we're on the other side of the Buzzard when this engine cranks; I can't guarantee a fan blade isn't going to go spinning away into the trees."

Derek got the damaged starboard engine started, and ran it up to five percent power. "The vibration isn't bad," he reported. "The dampeners are handling it."

"Run it up," Irene ordered. The engine was capable of running at 65% of its maximum power, before the vibration became unmanageable. "We'll keep it to 50% power," Irene suggested. "With the missing fan blades, the engine gives up only," she checked the remote control tablet, "35% of normal takeoff thrust. We lightened the bird," she glanced at the pile of seats, spare parts and everything else they had stripped out of the Buzzard. "We're good, it will fly."

"Yeah, like a wounded duck," Derek observed with a frown.

Irene bit her lip, studying the site where Major Perkins thought the Kristang had hidden some type of aircraft. "It's doable. What do you think?" She asked Derek. Irene had flown a Blackhawk transport helicopter on Earth, Derek had been an attack pilot.

"We can fly along this ravine," he traced a finger over the map, "it gives cover from the mountaintop. When we pop up over this ridge, we'll be right on top of whatever aircraft they have. We should have," he scratched his chin thoughtfully, "five seconds? From when we pop over the ridge to, um, impact."

Five seconds sounded like a long time to Perkins. "If the Kristang are ready for it, they'll shoot the Buzzard as soon as it clears the ridge."

"They won't know we're coming," Derek grinned with a wink. "We'll fly low and slow enough along the ravine, they won't see us, and they won't hear us. The starboard engine is surprisingly quiet until the throttle is at forty percent power, we'll keep it below that. This will work, Major," he looked up into Perkins' eyes. "How confident are you this spot is where they parked their aircraft?"

Perkins explained about the broken tree limbs.

"Yes, Ma'am," Derek agreed. "But if their pilots were smart, they would have set down there, dropped off their people and equipment, then flown to a better spot to park their bird."

Irene nodded. "That's what we would do."

Perkins suppressed a groan. She had been patting herself on the back for finding a stealthed alien aircraft, and her pilots were raining on her parade. "Shit. If that's the case, it could be anywhere." They would only get one shot at using their crippled Buzzard on a suicide mission. "We'll stick with the plan." Was that the smart thing to do? Forty thousand Ruhar, and the fate of humans on Paradise, might depend on whether she guessed correctly. "It's the best we can do."

They waited until Shauna sent a message that the drill bit was close to the powercells. Major Perkins shook her head in amazement at how short a time it had taken for the drill to reach that far through the volcanic rock of the island. Alien technology truly is incredible, she told herself. As soon as Shauna's signal was received, Perkins ordered the Buzzard to be started and sent on its last mission. As Derek Bonsu predicted, the unbalanced aircraft flew like a wounded duck.

What mattered was, it flew.

"Ahhhh, this narrow bandwidth signal is creating a serious time lag in the visuals," Irene warned, struggling with the remote control unit. "I'm having to trust the map and anticipate turns in the ravine, the images I'm getting are behind by almost a second. The portside engine almost clipped a rock a second ago," she said, her eyes hidden behind the virtual-reality goggles. In order to prevent the Kristang detecting the remote control commands Irene was sending to the Buzzard and the sensor data the Buzzard was sending back, they were using a very low-power, compressed signal that mimicked background noise. That was great for avoiding detection, but terrible for accuracy.

"Can you compensate?" Perkins asked anxiously. Shauna was holding the drill bit sixty meters from the powercells, fearful the Kristang had already discovered their activity. For the last twenty meters, the drill had been chewing through a vein of extra hard rock that required almost the full power of the drill; that hard rock would transmit vibrations the Kristang might detect.

"I am doing that, Ma'am," Irene tried to keep the annoyance from her voice. Since she was Irene, it didn't work. "With this lag, I won't know exactly where the ship will be when it crests the ridge. I'm going to let the autopilot guide it to crash after I pull it above the ridge."

"Use your best judgment," Perkins said tersely, fighting the knot in her stomach.

"What the hell are they doing?" Dave fumed. Being a soldier, he was used to standing by to stand by; sitting around doing nothing while waiting for someone else to get off their asses. By extraordinary herculean effort, which the US Army would consider 'doing their jobs', they had wrestled the drill rig up a partly dry streambed. Chopping branches off trees, fighting their way through dense underbrush that continuously snagged on the rig, and scratched the three humans and one adolescent Ruhar on every piece of exposed skin. Thorns that were especially thick poked right through their Army Combat Uniforms until they were all bloody here and there. All the time Dave had spent working with the drill rig had not changed his instinctive feeling that the six-legged machine was creepy. Watching it climb, its computer-guided legs almost intelligently feeling their way up the slope, had filled Dave with revulsion, as if the alien-built drill rig was a blood-thirsty insect crawling to bite him in half.

When they got the rig into position, they had drilled down, then forward, chewing through soil, fractured shale and solid volcanic rock until Shauna judged they were close enough to the powercells that any more drilling would be detected. Dave was all for punching through the final meters into the powercells, hooking up the surge inducer, and running like the wind.

But, no. Major Perkins ordered them to stand by, while she and their two pilots did-what? What the hell could the three of them do, with no weapons and a busted ship?

"Be patient, Ski," Jesse replied quietly. "The Major must have good reasons for whatever she's doing. She's been square with us all along."

"Hey, 'Pone, Perkins is good people, she's a grunt by association, but she's intel, not infantry. Our asses are hanging out to dry here," he looked fearfully at the sky. One of the reasons Shauna had chosen that location was, it could not be seen from the mountain peak that contained the maser projector. Dave considered at the moment that meant they couldn't see if the Kristang were coming for them.

"Dave, it's above our pay grade," Shauna said over her shoulder as she finished hooking up their hand-made surge inducer.

"We get paid?" Dave said with mock surprise.

"You know what she means, Ski." Jesse wasn't any happier about the delay that Dave was. "Uh, Shauna, is there anything we can do now, so we can move faster once we get the 'Go' order?"

The two Kristang pilots, happy to be exempted from the dirty, rough and dangerous duty of clearing a path down to the projector, were sitting in the cockpit of their Jawkuar, monitoring the condition of the all-important stealth and jamming fields. Behind them in the passenger compartment, the side door was open, allowing a breeze to circulate, because the dropship's environmental control systems were offline. The pilots were speculating on what sort of poem would be appropriate to commemorate killing forty thousand of their hated enemy. The commando leader would of course officially be responsible for composing the poem himself, but he typically welcomed input from his team. To have one's poem selected by the leader was a great honor.

"We stood unseen, shrouded by-" the lead pilot paused in the composition of his poem. "What is that sound?"

"What sound?" The other pilot strained to hear. Neither of the pilots had served on Paradise before they arrived with Admiral Kekrando's battlegroup, and they were not familiar with the native life on the planet, particularly whatever animals lived in the tropics. With the steady trade winds rustling the dry palm fronds and whistling through the open door, it was difficult to pick out one sound. "I don't-" Then he heard it. A whining sound, faint, increasing in pitch. It was getting closer. And suddenly, it became a screaming roar, as the Buzzard cleared the ridge and increased power into a dive.

The Buzzard's autopilot had been programmed to aim for the center of the clearing; aiming at nothing but grass, low-growing shrubs and scattered rocks according to its stealth-blinded sensors. The Jawkuar was parked toward the east side of the clearing, so the nose of the Buzzard missed the enemy dropship entirely and buried itself in the rich volcanic soil. The remainder of the Buzzard followed its own nose, and exploded, tearing the Jawkuar apart and causing that dropship's own powercells to explode.

"Whoa!" Irene exclaimed, pointing to black smoke and a mushroom-like, roiling ball of fire rising into the sky on the mountain peak. The actual crash site was not visible from the beach; it didn't need to be. "I think you were right, Major. That explosion is from something more than our little Buzzard." As she spoke, another ball of fire rose into the air, twisting in the wind. "Yup, those are secondaries for sure. We hit something, whatever it was."

"That's what it looks like to me, too. Striebich, Bonsu, that's good work. Sorry about your aircraft; I'll see if I can get you a new one. Let's launch these boats and pick up the others." Dragging a boat down to the water with one hand, she called Dave on her zPhone. "Czajka, get that drill going. When it punches through to the powercells, set it up for a power overload, and the four of you pop smoke down to the beach. We'll have the boats waiting for you."

"Done. There, it's set," Shauna announced, looking up from the drill rig's console. She held up her zPhone. "I can trigger the overload from my zPhone. Major Perkins has the same capability." Slapping the cover of the console shut, she reached under, pulled a lever to release the console, and tossed it on the ground. "Who wants to do it?"

"Do what?" Jesse asked.

"Smash it," Shauna explained, hands on her hips, the expression on her face implying a 'duh' she didn't say aloud. "So if the lizards get here before we trigger the overload, they won't be able to operate the drill. We can't let them screw with the surge inducer."

"Oh," Jesse's face reddened. It was obvious, now that he thought about it. He stooped and picked up a large rock. "As much of a royal pain in the ass this drill rig has been, I'm going to miss it. Feels like a member of the team by now. Y'all stand back." He heaved the rock overhead with both hands, and swung it down to bash the console. "Dagnabit!" The console's casing cracked, but it was still intact. He tried again with the rock, and this time the console broke in two pieces. "That did it. We are outa here."

"Uh, Shauna, we have a complication?" Dave replied. "Nert wants to stay here, to make sure the powercells overload."

Oh, great, Shauna thought, while mentally kicking herself. She should have anticipated the young Ruhar cadet would not like the idea of running away from the drill rig before he could be certain it had completed its job. "Nert, I understand you want to be absolutely certain the Kristang can't shoot those transport ships," she said softly. "We don't need to be here to do that. I can overload the powercells remotely," she waved her zPhone.

Nert's chin bobbed up and down in nervous agreement. "What if the Kristang come here and disable the surge inducer, before you trigger the overload?" The young man's words sounded stilted and formal, coming through the translator. He had seen the surge inducer device the three humans had cobbled together from the drill's power supply, and he was not confident it would work. The real problem is he did not trust three backward, primitive humans to operate technology. The lives of almost forty thousand Ruhar depended on *him*. "They could disconnect the power supply from here."

Shauna could see Nert's fear, the expression was clear even on an alien face. The boy almost had tears welling in his eyes. "Nert, we thought of that, remember? Dave and Jesse installed something we humans call a 'booby trap'." She paused to see if Nert understood whatever that phrase translated to in the common Ruhar language. Recognition dawned on Nert's face, so she continued. "If anyone tampers with the power connection, the surge triggers automatically. Even if the Kristang blow up his whole drill rig somehow, the power surge will be delivered."

Nert's mouth formed a silent 'O'. Without using his zPhone translator, he spoke. "It goes boom?"

"Oh, yeah," Dave put his hands together, then flung them apart. "*Big* badda boom! Like, this whole island, kid. We need to make like a shepherd, and get the flock outa here."

Jesse snorted with laughter. "Nert, he means we need to leave right now." Twelve minutes had passed since the Buzzard crashed on its suicide run, and Major Perkins had ordered the drill to punch through the final distance into the projector's powercells. By now, it was likely the Kristang had figured out what was going on, and were frantically on their way to the drill rig site.

Nert still hesitated, so Jesse tried another tactic. Major Perkins would not be pleased if they didn't bring their young Ruhar liaison officer with them. "Cadet, our mission here is complete. Someone needs to report to your command what happened here."

Whether that made sense to Nert, or he was simply happy for a reasonable excuse, he nodded vigorously. "We go now?"

Nert, even at easy jogging speed, reached the beach before the three humans. He raced the final hundred meters, bounding along the broken terrain, waving his arms and shouting. Major Perkins waved him toward her boat. "Cadet, where are the others?"

"Behind me," Nert pointed back along the stream bed. To the annoyance of Perkins, the young Ruhar was not breathing hard. Her three young fit soldiers stumbled onto the beach two minutes later, breathing raggedly, faces red from exertion.

"Czajka, you're with me," Perkins ordered. They launched both boats in the gentle surf, and motored out toward the fringing reef. Perkins had been studying the waves breaking over the reef, and had planned a path through the reef. Irene's boat, with Derek, Shauna, and Jesse aboard, was almost tipped over by a breaking wave, but she powered over the crest and into the open sea. Both boats went to full power, headed for the west side of the closest island.

"I'm still not getting a signal from outside, Ma'am," Dave reported, playing with his zPhone. "Whatever jamming field the lizards are using, it covers more than that one island. Should we trigger the power surge now?"

Perkins, who was steering the raft, looked ahead. They were approaching the other island, but she wanted to go around the back side, and beach the boats there. If a tsunami hit where they were, it could carry the two boats high up to crash into the island's near shore. "Not yet. I want to get us around this point first."

"Yes, Ma'am, I understand that," Dave said with a frown. "I'm worried that this jamming field could interfere with our zPhone connection with the drill rig. When you called us there, the signal had a lot of static."

Perkins looked at Dave sharply. Why the hell had he not mentioned that concern earlier? "Czajka," she let out a breath, annoyed. "Is there a way you can tell on that phone, the strength of the signal connection to the drill rig?"

Dave's eyebrows raised. "Uh, I can, uh, check on that." Shit, he mentally kicked himself, *I should have thought of that.* "There must be a-"

There was a bright flash from behind them, then the mountaintop erupted like the extinct volcano coming back to life. Dave only had enough time to open his mouth in shock, before his view of the exploding peak was obscured by a dust cloud, and the entire island rippled. At first Dave thought the ripple was the ground shaking, until he realized the ripple was in the *air*. It was a shockwave, headed straight for them. Then the whole mountain exploded, sending rock upward and outward.

"Shit!" Dave shouted, his face white. "They must have triggered the booby trap! How the hell did the lizards get there so fast?"

Perkins ignored his question, yanking on Dave's top. "Down!" She shouted so her voice could be heard by the other boat, where Irene had already ordered everyone to lay flat in the bottom of the boat. Emily had barely enough time to throw herself prone and cover her ears when the bone-shaking roar swept over them, followed by a prolonged, low, rolling thunder. Perkins was about to raise her head when the shockwave hit, and the boat was flipped over, sending her cartwheeling across the waves. Impact with the water jarred her and she briefly lost consciousness, coming back to reality laying face up, supported by the Ruhar life vest that had automatically inflated. The vest included a blinking light and emergency locator beacon, and some gizmo that kept ocean predators away. Coughing up seawater, she looked around frantically for the others. Dave floated a mere twenty feet away from her, holding onto Nert whose eyes were closed. To her other side, Derek waved a hand weakly and gave her a thumbs up on behalf of the others. The boats had flipped over and tumbled in the shockwave, with the closest one now fifty meters away.

"Dave- Czajka!" She remembered decorum a little too late. "How is Nert?" As she shouted, the Ruhar cadet's eyes opened, and he nodded his head at Dave.

"Good!" Dave whispered, or it seemed to Perkins that he whispered, because her hearing was recovering from the shockwave. Dave saw she had trouble hearing, or his own hearing was affected also. "He is good," he shouted slowly, giving her a thumbs up.

Nert blinked, heaved, and coughed up seawater and whatever he had last eaten. "I Ok," he said, embarrassed. Then his eyes grew wide, and he pointed toward where the projector island had been. Most of the island above a dozen feet above the water was gone, although there was so much smoke, ash and steam not much could be seen. What could be seen were huge chunks of the island splashing into the sea, with some rocks flying toward and even beyond Perkins and her team.

But what had truly scared Nert was the wave. "No good!" He exclaimed in squeaky English. "No is good!"

"Ya think?" Dave replied without thinking. Unlike in movies, this tsunami was not a vertical, breaking wave. The entire surface of the sea had risen a dozen feet as was rushing toward them, with the front boiling foam.

"Hang-" Was all Perkins had time to say, before she was engulfed. The first part was not as bad as she feared, being like a wave you might body surf at the beach, then the wall of water hit like a concrete wall.

CHAPTER NINE

In one way, the tsunami did Major Perkins and her team a favor; the massive surge of water lifted them up high over the jagged coral reef fringing the island they had been headed for. The wave carried them along; sometimes above the surface, sometimes being tumbled over and over in the water. Emily recalled keeping her head above the water three times, gasping for air; most of the time it seemed like she was underwater even with the Ruhar life vest doing its best to keep her upright and above the surface.

The tsunami swept over the island, and climbed high into the hills, breaking trees along the way. Perkins and her team had the good fortune to be carried over a peninsula that jutted out from the island, separating two half-moon shaped beaches. The second beach encompassed a broad, deep-bottomed bay; going from shallow water to deep water dissipated part of the tsunami's force.

Emily didn't know how long she was in the water or what happened along the way. She was battered by strong waves and scraped against the sandy bottom of the bay and coral and debris and turned around and around so many times, she barely knew who she was. What she did know was that after a while, she felt someone hugging her from behind, and an arm around her chest. "Major, it's me, Czajka. I've got you."

She vomited up seawater, choking and gasping. When she could finally speak, she could only manage a strangled "Dave."

"It's me, it's me," he whispered in her ear. Or he was shouting and her ears were too full of water to hear properly. "You're ok, you're ok. Everyone made it." He waved a hand to Shauna, who was helping Derek get to shore. Jesse, Irene and Nert were already on the debris-choked beach, coughing up seawater. Broken palm trees were scattered across the beach like matchsticks, or bobbing in the still-sloshing water of the bay.

"Everyone? Safe?"

"Yes, we all made it," Dave assured her.

"I can move," Perkins protested, embarrassed.

"I can help you," Dave said gently.

"Let me try," she said, and as he released his arm, she found her arms and legs still worked, although everything was stiff and sore. She turned to face Dave. "Thank you," she said simply, regretting that the rank structure prevented her from saying more.

Dave grinned, the grin of those surprised and happy to be alive. "No problem, Major. Watch out for that tree."

Side by side, neither of them swimming swiftly, they made their way through the floating debris to the shore. Emily's boots touched the sandy bottom, and as she splashed her way up to the beach in her soaked uniform, she could not help indulging herself. Holding a hand to her lips as if smoking a pipe and striking a dramatic pose, she pointed to the shattered projector island. "I shall *not* return."

That remark broke everyone into laughter, except for Nert, who of course had never heard of Douglas MacArthur.

Satisfied for the moment that no one had life-threatening injuries, she moved on to the next issue. "Does anyone still have a zPhone?" Perkins patted her pockets in dismay. Her zPhone had been in the left breast pocket of her blouse; a pocket that had been torn away, only a scrap of the flap remained.

"No."

"I lost mine."

"Me too."

Craig Alanson

"I've got, oh," Irene held up her credit-card-thin zPhone, which was now bent at a forty five degree angle. "I didn't know these things could bend."

"Or break," Dave held up the two pieces of his shattered zPhone.

"Nert?" Perkins asked hopefully.

The Ruhar cadet shook his head. Without zPhones to translate, he had to use his very limited English. "I not had that," he said with an awkward grin.

"Hell," Perkins expressed her dismay. "We have no way to contact the Ruhar?"

"The emergency locator beacons on our boats will be transmitting, Ma'am," Irene said with as much cheer as she could muster. One of the orange boats could be seen floating, upside down, just beyond the reef. The important fact was that it was still floating.

"The beacons only tell the Ruhar an aircraft went down here, and they already know that. What I'm worried about is the Ruhar thinking there might still be a threat here, and saturating this entire area with railgun darts," Perkins explained in exasperation.

"Oh, shit," Irene looked down shamefacedly. "I hadn't thought of that."

"I hope the *Ruhar* don't think of that. Does anyone have a serious injury?" Perkins asked. Her left knee hurt, causing her to limp. It felt like it she turned it to the right at all, something important would snap. Everyone had cuts, bumps, deep scrapes, bruises and what Perkins thought were mild sprains. Everyone was bleeding here and there, none of it immediately serious. Derek had the worst injury; his left wrist was hanging at an awkward angle and he had three broken fingers on that hand. "We'll survive," Perkins concluded. "The Ruhar will either hit us from orbit, or send a dropship. Either way, it won't take long."

"Hey, Shauna," Dave said with a cough, pounding his chest to get the seawater out. "Let's overload the powercells, you said. That was a *great* idea."

"Did you have to blow up the *entire* freakin' island?" Derek complained with a grin.

"Yeah, sorry about that," Shauna own voice echoed in her head, because of the water in her ears. She tilted her head to one side to get the water out, but it only sloshed around. She suspected she would be picking sand out of her hair and other places for days.

"Hey, it worked," Jesse felt the need to defend his sort-of girlfriend.

"It did," Irene grimaced at her sore shoulder. "Next time, let's try for a solution in the sub-megaton range, huh?"

"I'll remember that," Shauna kept shaking her head, and the water in her ears kept sloshing. "Ah, there's more sand in my clothes than on this beach."

Perkins felt rubbed raw by the sandpaper-like grit between her clothes and skin. "Me too. Jarrett, Striebich, we need to get these clothes off and rinse them out. We don't need more sand getting in cuts." Rivulets of blood trickling down her cheek and dripping on her neck. At least the blood was flushing sand out of the cuts. "You men," she looked at Derek, Jesse, Dave and Nert, "go around the corner to that other beach. Meet back here in twenty."

Jesse, Dave and Derek waited with Nert, discretely peering over the pile of broken trees and other debris to see if the three women had finished washing the sand off their skin and were back on the beach. The three men and the alien boy called out, before walking from their bay to where the women were standing in the sun, trying to get their clothes dry while wearing them.

"That is not fair," Irene pointed at the shirtless men, as Derek hung his shirt on a broken tree branch to dry in the steady breeze. "My shirt is so encrusted with salt, it itches."

Trouble on Paradise

"You have a bra on," Derek almost snapped at her, his broken wrist starting to throb and making him grumpy. "You don't need to wear a shirt for me."

For a second, Irene considered removing her shirt, as she was wearing a jogging bra, and after all they were on a tropical beach. There was no real difference between wearing a bra and wearing a bikini top. Major Perkins clearly had no intention of letting the men under her command see her walking around in a bra, so Irene sighed. "Maybe later."

Without her asking, Jesse picked up Shauna's boots, which had become half filled with sand and broken bits of shell. "I'll clean these out for you," he offered, turning the boots upside down and bashing them together. Sand, shells, seawater, splintered wood and one wriggling little sea creature spilled out.

"Oh!" Nert exclaimed, pointing excitedly. "*That* is what 'knocking boots' means!"

"What?" Jesse's face turned red. "It's not-"

Shauna hushed him with a waving hand. "Yes, Nert, that is what 'knocking boots' means. Cornpone, Jesse," she blushed, "is showing he cares for me by cleaning my boots."

"Ah," the alien boy nodded with sudden understanding. In halting English, he asked "this is a prelude to mating?"

"Nert!" Jesse spoke quickly to get the Ruhar cadet to shut up. "That is not-"

"Maybe," Shauna said quietly with a wink toward Jesse. "If Jesse keeps his mouth shut."

"Mmm," Nert grinned.

"Less talking, more cleaning." Jesse waded out into the water, plunging Shauna's boots under the water to get the rest of the sand out. "While I'm out here, y'all toss your boots to me, and I'll clean them." More cleaning, less talking. Jesse was going to clean everything in sight, if he had to.

Captain Rastall clenched his fists tightly to release some of his nervous energy. Outwardly, he was calm, in cool command of his ship and crew. Inwardly, he chafed at further delays in what had been a long and tedious chase of the hidden enemy ship. If left to himself, Rastall would have preferred the *Mem Hertall* to go in alone, maser cannons blazing and missiles running hot. That would be eminently satisfying, to see an enemy ship panic, drop stealth and attempt to accelerate away. That would also be giving the enemy a chance to escape, and potentially to end Rastall's promising career. So, instead of giving in to emotion and acting rashly, he waited for the tightbeam laser signal from the *Grathur*. The *Toman* had signaled minutes ago that ship was ready. As soon as all three ships, wrapped tightly in stealth fields, indicated they were ready, he would initiate the attack.

Behind Rastall, the communications officer spoke. "Captain, signal received from the *Grathur*, she is in position and waiting your order."

"Status?" Rastall asked, though on his own display, he could see status of all vital shipboard systems.

"All systems ready," the first officer reported.

"Initiate countdown," Rastall ordered without hesitation. Although all three Ruhar ships were in stealth, using only passive sensors, he worried the enemy could detect their transmissions. The ships had crisscrossed the area, with the *Hertall* continuing to follow the trail of particles left behind by the ghost ship, and the other two ships determining the trail ended ahead of the *Hertall*. Somewhere out there, somewhere close, was a stealthed enemy ship. It puzzled Rastall and his sensor experts that a Kristang ship that close had not yet been detected, for stealth was not usually a strength of Kristang technology.

Rastall had taken a risk in ordering his ship to maneuver away from the particle trail, so the area ahead was between the *Hertall* and the star. He was hoping his ship's passive sensors could detect a ripple where the enemy's stealth field bent the star's light around the ship. That technique was known to be quite effective against most enemy ships. Had the Kristang developed, or more likely bought or stolen, advanced stealth technology? If so, discovering the characteristics of such a new stealth field would be more important than destroying a single enemy ship that threatened a populated planet.

"Both ships acknowledged," the first officer reported. "Countdown coordinated and running. Four, three, two, one, activate!"

The *Mem Hertall*, hidden and painfully quiet while acting as a passive sensor platform for far too long, came to life as a warship. Simultaneously with the two other ships, the *Hertall* dropped her stealth field and extended both an active sensor field to pinpoint the enemy's location, and a damping field to prevent the enemy from jumping away. Each of the three ships launched a pair of missiles, initially unguided. The missiles were targeted at the area where the enemy ship was most likely hiding. Once each missile's mothership locked in the enemy's exact position with a sensor field, targeting coordinates were passed to the missiles. The missiles changed course and surged forward at maximum acceleration. Only seconds remained in the enemy ship's life.

"No response?" Captain Rastall asked anxiously. Despite his strong desire to see the destruction of an enemy ship that had tormented him for months, he hoped the Kristang would see the hopelessness of their situation and surrender. Because the enemy ship had not declared itself at the time of the ceasefire agreement, the ship was not covered by the agreement, and therefore would not be allowed to simply be transported away by the Jeraptha. Rastall could seize and board the enemy ship, learn its secrets, take its crew prisoner to be exchanged for Ruhar prisoners later. Capturing the *Glory* would be more of a triumph than simply destroying that ship.

"No," the first officer's voice reflected puzzlement. "The enemy is not reacting in any way, Captain. No change in status, and they haven't dropped their stealth field."

"Could their crew be dead?" Rastall speculated.

"That is unlikely? We know the ship has been maneuvering," they could tell because the particle trail had curved and swung back and forth while they followed it. "And not randomly. It hasn't been drifting, or spinning around by a malfunctioning thruster. Someone has been directing its flight."

Rastall had a terrible thought. "Or some*thing*." Had they been chasing a dead ship, directed only by its AI?

"Your orders?" The first officer glanced at the tactical display. The first missile was almost on top of the enemy ship.

Rastall took a moment to think. The reason they had fired missiles instead of masers is because incoming missiles gave the enemy time to surrender. And because missiles could be recalled. Rastall could order the missiles to self-destruct, or simply deactivate. "Let the first missile run, put the other five into a holding pattern."

The first missile, its seeker being fed targeting data by all three ships, raced in toward the target. When it was six seconds from impact, the missile switched on its own active sensors, risking detection and interception by the enemy ship's defensive maser turrets. The missile was prepared to be fired on by maser cannons; if its computer determined the missile would be destroyed, it would explode its shaped-charge warhead in the direction of the enemy ship.

The missile was not intercepted, it had the unusual privilege of impacting the enemy ship directly before exploding.

Trouble on Paradise

"Detonation confirmed," the first officer reported. Then he frowned, rechecked the data, and frowned more deeply. "Captain, there was no secondary explosion. The debris field is barely large enough to be a," he groaned as the truth dawned on him, "a *dropship*."

"We've been following a *dropship*?" Rastall asked, incredulous.

"Or something roughly that size, based on the debris."

"How? We have been following radioactive particles. Hull coating that we know is from the *Glory*. How could-" Rastall knew the answer to his own question. The crew of the *Glory* must have scraped off a section of their ship's hull coating, and put the particles into a container, along with oxygen, radioactive reactor waste. Then the container sprayed its contents slowly, creating a trail that appeared to be coming from a battle-damaged Kristang frigate. The *Hertall* and the other two ships had been chasing a decoy. Rastall slammed a fist down on a console and shouted a Ruhar curse word. "Where is the *Glory*?!"

Satisfied that the Ruhar guard ships were following the decoy, the frigate *To Seek Glory in Battle is Glorious* had slowly maneuvered to within twenty seven lightminutes of the planet they knew as Pradassis. Her captain planned that maneuver to monitor Ruhar guard ship movements around the planet, before the overworked little ship had to make its final two jumps into low orbit, to pick up 39 Commando's Jawkuar. Those might be the ship's final two jumps ever, in her captain's opinion. Although the Ruhar's strategic defense satellite network around Pradassis had barely begun construction, and the battlegroup was away on a fleet exercise, the Ruhar guard ships were on patrol, ever watchful.

Twenty seven lightminutes, which was the equivalent of a nice round, lucky number in the Kristang numbering system, was far enough away so the *Glory* would not be in serious danger from the guard ships. If the battlegroup had been in orbit, frigates might have been sent out to investigate the gamma ray burst of the *Glory* jumping in. Without support from the fleet, the guard ships were not going to be lured away from orbit. Or so the *Glory*'s captain hoped. He checked the sensor displays, finding everything at Pradassis was as he expected them to be. Or at least, they had been that way, twenty seven minutes ago. He checked the clock. There was no point delaying any longer, it would too soon be time to jump into whatever Fate had in mind for the ship that had pushed its luck far too many times already. He turned away from the sensor display, and resignedly slumped into his command chair. "Program jump drive for-"

"Captain!" Second Officer Smando called out. "There has been an explosion."

"In orbit?" The captain asked, gripping the arms of his chair. The special forces warriors of 39 Commando had timed their rendezvous with the *Glory* precisely to occur just after the maser projector destroyed the two Ruhar transport ships. An explosion now would throw off all their plans, and make it extremely difficult for the *Glory* to pick up the commandos. But, the timing also did not make sense. When the captain checked mere moments ago, the two Ruhar transports were still maneuvering to match course and speed with the top of the space elevator, and one of the transports was still behind the planet. Had the commandos been forced to act early, and attack only one transport?

"No," Smando was puzzled. "On the surface."

The captain leapt out of his chair to stand beside Smando, and checked the coordinates of the explosion. "That's a projector site," he muttered, almost to himself.

"What do you think it means, Captain?"

"I think," the captain answered with a wryly bemused smile, "that 39 Commando will be late for the rendezvous." He looked directly at Smando. "*Very* late."

"Oh. *Oh*," Smando said as the implication dawned on him. "That's *the* projector site." He knew the broad outlines on 39 Commando's plan, but not the details. "They blew it up?" That surely could not have been part of the plan.

"Or it blew up on them by accident," the captain mused. "They were attempting to reactivate an old projector, without the proper equipment or training." Neither of them considered that a third party may have blown up the site, and 39 Commando with it. They certainly never imagined that lowly humans could have been involved.

"What should we do now?" Smando asked.

"Now?" The captain sat down in his chair again. "We send a distress call to the Ruhar."

"Sir?"

"Smando, it is unfortunate that our extensive battle damage has, until recently, rendered our communications systems and jump drive inoperable," the captain shook his head sadly. "That is why Admiral Kekrando thought we had been destroyed, and why we missed being transported back home by the Jeraptha. Now that our heroic repair efforts have been successful, we are complying with the cease fire terms and reporting our presence to the Ruhar."

Smando caught on quickly. "I regret to report that the battle damage also affected our computer systems, so that no useful data exists about our recent activities."

"That is unfortunate indeed," the captain nodded gravely. "I commend our technical staff for keeping the ship operational, despite the severe damage to our computer systems."

"I will convey your admiration to the technical staff," Smando bowed, wondering just how big an explosive would be needed to wipe out the ship's computing center. The technical staff should know that sort of thing.

Several minutes later, the second officer was at the chief engineer's duty station. "You want me to blow it up?" The chief engineer asked incredulously.

"I know you and your people have worked miracles to keep the computers operating this long, so it would be a shame to-"

"No! No, sir, I would love to blow up that obsolete piece of junk," the chief engineer said gleefully. "I may reward my team by letting them smash it with hammers," he considered, talking mostly to himself. "Is there anything else on this decrepit pile of crap that I can blow up or destroy before the Ruhar arrive? That would prevent Fleet from telling me to keep the equipment going somehow."

"Just the computer core for now," Smando cautioned. "However," he said with a wide grin, "I will ask the captain about other systems. He may wish for you to render the entire structure unsalvageable. This ship's luck should have run out a long time ago."

Major Perkins had just rinsed her feet and pulled her newly-cleaned boots back on, before a pair of aircraft flashed overhead, followed by a sonic boom that rattled her teeth. The aircraft, mere dark streaking dots in the sky, curved around to circle where the projector island had been. Irene helped Perkins stand steady while she pulled her boots on, watching a rapidly-approaching dark spot, high in the sky. The dot grew into a Ruhar dropship; it slowed and circled the island as the six humans and one Ruhar cadet waved their arms in a manner intended to be friendly. Perkins hoped the sharp imagers of the dropship would see Nert, in his battered Ruhar cadet's uniform, and determine the little group on the beach was not hostile.

"Uh, oh," Irene announced. "They're coming in to land."

"Why is that an 'uh oh'?" Jesse asked.

Irene and Derek glanced at each other. "Because," Irene explained, pointing left and right along the beach, "this beach isn't anywhere near big enough for that dropship to land."

To Irene's relief, the dropship's pilot knew that. The big ship hovered over the water, safely offshore, and a door opened. A Ruhar dressed in some sort of slick coveralls was lowered into the water on a thin cable, and headed toward shore, propelled by a thing like a short surfboard with a motor.

"Now *that's* a cool toy," Jesse said admiringly.

The new Ruhar reached the shore and removed its helmet, revealing a young fuzzy-faced woman. Perkins recognized the rank insignia as *klasta*, roughly equivalent to a lieutenant. Perkins saluted and her team followed, but the wary klasta ignored the humans and spoke to Nert.

Nert said something, and pointed to Perkins, so the klasta pulled out two devices like small zPhones, and handed one to Perkins. The klasta spoke into her device. "What happened here?"

Emily Perkins took a deep breath. "How much time do you have?"

CHAPTER TEN

Deputy Administrator, technically now acting Chief Administrator, Baturnah Logellia stood up when Emily Perkins was escorted into the office. "Major Perkins, it is good to see you." She offered a warm handshake, not being squeamish about touching the strange aliens. "Please, sit." When Perkins had sat down, Baturnah pushed a ceramic cup and a covered pot across the table, along with a small box. "Would you like co-ffee?" She pronounced the unfamiliar alien word. Tapping the box, she added, "or choc-o-late?"

"Coffee?" Perkins' eyes grew wide. "*Chocolate*?" She had not tasted coffee in, she could not remember back that far. Her last bite of chocolate had been during the mission for Emby, and that had been a small piece of Hershey bar that was long past its sell-by date. "Where did you get this?" She asked with suspicion and guilt. Suspicion, because UNEF HQ had long suspected the Ruhar had a secret stash of human food from Earth. Guilt, because drinking or eating items from that secret stash would be betraying the entire Expeditionary Force, trapped as they were over a thousand lightyears from Earth.

"We made it," Baturnah beamed pride. "Your word is syn-the-size," she said carefully. "Our scientists analyzed the chemical structure of these foods, they are confident they have created a reasonable approximation of these items."

Perkins poured herself a half cup, thinking that no matter how terrible it tasted, she could swallow half a cup without gagging. "Hmm. Hmmm," she hummed, pleasantly surprised. The coffee was bitter, in a pot-sat-too-long-on-the-burner kind of way. Typical coffee in any Army office around the USA. Or in any gas station convenience store. She smacked her lips quietly. Something about the flavor was slightly off, until she realized the Ruhar had tried to add vanilla to the brew. Maybe the vanilla was there to mask deficiencies in the overall blend? "Administrator-"

"Please, call me Baturnah, Major Perkins. We have known each other some time now, and often not under official circumstances."

"I will call you Baturnah, if you call me Emily," Perkins replied with what she intended as a charming smile."

"Yes, Emily."

"This is good," Perkins lifted her cup of ersatz coffee. "It's not perfect, but everyone's taste is different."

"Please, try the chocolate," Baturnah requested, eager to see if her scientists had been successful with that concoction. They had warned her that, while 'chocolate' was a favorite treat of humans, it was a very complex mixture of subtle flavors and mouth feel.

Opening the box, Perkins found twelve small cubes of chocolate, of a light brown color she guessed had been modelled after milk chocolate. She popped one in her mouth and let it melt on her tongue. It was surprisingly good! "Thank you, I," she popped another in her mouth before she could think about it. It had been a long time since she tasted chocolate. "This is very good, just as it is. Please, offer my thanks to your scientists."

"I will. The scientists actually work for the fleet; they created this coffee and chocolate as a gift from Admiral Mohvalu. The Admiral is extremely grateful for your actions at Tavalen Island."

"We performed our duty," Perkins said simply.

"Please, Emily, do not be so modest. My nephew gave me a full report, in person. The actions of your team saved the lives of forty thousand Ruhar. My people, and myself, owe you a great debt. Because of your actions, and the fact that I am now the acting Chief Administrator," the former chief had formally resigned and was awaiting transfer back home, "the public perception of UNEF has changed. Most people on Gehtanu are related to, or knew, someone on those two transport ships. Most of my people here would be mourning their loss, if not for the bravery of your team. Your team is not being disbanded, although there are few projector sites remaining to be reactivated, so we will need give you a new assignment. I was thinking your team could train with a Ruhar infantry unit, to learn our tactics and equipment. You could observe and advise us, and then your team could select and participate in the training of other humans, to serve alongside Ruhar security teams. If, that is, you choose to accept."

"Yes," Perkins said without hesitation. "Yes, we would be honored. Thank you, Administrator."

"You would be serving what I believe your people call 'dirtside' at first, here on Gehtanu. Later, depending on circumstances," she smiled, sure that Perkins would understand, "some humans might be offered the opportunity to serve as Fleet Marines aboard a starship. Admiral Mohvalu and his staff are favorably impressed by the quick thinking and inventiveness of your team. Using a drill to penetrate the powercells of that projector," she smiled broadly, "was impressive thinking. Our intelligence people are also impressed that you located a stealthed Jawkuar dropship."

I got lucky. Perkins kept that thought to herself. "Thank you. Will, um, this new public attitude toward humans-"

"Toward UNEF," Baturnah corrected. "Not all humans. Not Keepers."

"I understand," Perkins nodded. To hell with those Sleeper idiots. "Will this new perception of UNEF result in us not being relocated to southern Lemuria?"

"No," Baturnah answered sadly. "That project has acquired too much momentum." Buildings and roads and water systems were already being constructed to create new settlements for humans. "I did ask General Singh," the current UNEF commander, "about the issue, and he assured me the more temperate climate of southern Lemuria is preferable to the jungles your people currently occupy. However, the timetable for the movement has been relaxed, and some of your people can remain in the jungles, if they choose to do so. We will also be allowing your people to fly their own transport aircraft, and operate cargo ships."

That sounded like a win-win situation to Perkins.

"Thank you, Baturnah."

"I do have two additional requests of you," the Burgermeister said with a broad smile. "First, my nephew Nert has requested leave from school, to remain with your team. Serving as your liaison officer has been good for him, I would like him to continue with you, if you approve."

"Agreed. Nert is a fine young man, and he has been very useful. Your second request?"

"Emily, could you perhaps try to ensure that your team's future activities are not so," she searched for the correct English word, "*eventful?*"

Eric Koblenz flinched at the loud clanging sound, as the dropship detached from the cradle in the transport ship's docking bay. Three days after the Jeraptha star carriers jumped away from Paradise, they had rendezvoused with a Thuranin star carrier, and the Keepers had transferred to a Kristang troop transport ship. Kristang soldiers had herded humans into very cramped quarters aboard the transport. Food and even water had been in short supply, and the attitude of the Kristang crew anything but friendly. Eric was not the only Keeper fearing that he had made a huge mistake leaving Paradise. After many jumps and at least one transition through a wormhole, the transport ship had left the star carrier and maneuvered for almost an hour. Then Eric and three hundred of his fellow Keepers had been roughly shoved into a dropship; Eric was bleeding from where a Kristang had jabbed him with the muzzle of a rifle to hurry him along.

Although Eric was squashed in against the hull of the filthy dropship, and the air circulation was poor, he at least was next to one of only four tiny windows. As the dropship cleared the transport ship's docking bay, a harsh shaft of intense sunlight shone through the dirty, scuffed window. Eric blinked and shaded his eyes with a hand.

When his eyes adjusted, he peered out the window. The dropship fired thrusters and rotated, bringing a planet into view. Eric gasped.

"What the hell are we doing *here*?"

THE END

The Expeditionary Force series
Book 1: Columbus Day
Book 2: SpecOps
Book 3: Paradise
Book '3.5': Trouble on Paradise novella
Book 4: Black Ops
Book 5: Zero Hour- coming November 2017

Contact the author at craigalanson@gmail.com

https://www.facebook.com/Craig.Alanson.Author/

Go to craigalanson.com for blogs and ExForce logo merchandise including T-shirts, patches, sticker, hats, and coffee mugs

Made in the USA
Lexington, KY
12 April 2018